**Here's what critics are saying about
Erin Huss's books:**

"You cannot help but fall in love with Cambria!"
~ *Cozy Mystery Book Reviews*

"There is so much to love about this series Clever and
entertaining! Erin Huss has a delightful writing style...I
highly recommend this series!"
~ *Kings River Life Magazine*

"This enchanting novel has hit a home run. I would highly
recommend this book to anyone seeking a fun adventure
with a bit of danger tossed in for fun."
~ *Night Owl Reviews*

"An unforgettable story with plenty of oddball
characters...uproariously funny."
 ~ *InD'Tale Magazine*

"Hilarious and fun!"
~ *The Huffington Post*

D1714278

Books by Erin Huss:

Cambria Clyne Mysteries:

"Strawberry Swirl & Suspicion "
(short story in the Pushing Up Daisies collection)

French Vanilla & Felonies

Rocky Road & Revenge

Double Fudge & Danger

Mint Chip & Murder

MINT CHIP & MURDER

_____

a Cambria Clyne mystery

Erin Huss

*To Ashlyn & Emma, my two favorite aspiring authors.
Keep writing!*

Acknowledgements:

A big thank you to Gemma Halliday, Susie Halliday, and everyone at GHP. To Jed, Natalie, Noah, Emma, Ryder, and Fisher, you are my motivation. Thank you to Paula Bothwell for your beta and editing—you're the best!

PROLOGUE

———

We all make mistakes. You know it. I know it. Every nineties teenager who spent a decade over-plucking their eyebrows knows it, too. Some mistakes are small. Like when you accidentally set your alarm for p.m. instead of a.m. and wake up late. Some are inconvenient. Like when you forget to take the trash cans out and have to live with smelly garbage for a full week.

There are the bigger mistakes. Like, *oops*, I forgot to take my birth control pill (hello, baby), or miscalculated the month's expense report (goodbye, bonus), or used the expired meat for dinner instead of throwing it away (hello, food poisoning).

Then there are the catastrophic mistakes. The mistakes that destroys lives, or even end them.

This is what makes my job *interesting*. As an apartment manager, I'm privy to all my residents' freak flags, secrets, fears, and mistakes. Whether I want to be or not.

Trust me. It's not a job for the easily annoyed, argumentative, or anyone prone to migraines. It's a job for me...or at least I thought it was.

I made a whopper of a mistake, and I'm not sure anything or anyone will ever be the same.

CHAPTER ONE

Cambria J. Clyne
Highly motivated property manager seeking to take next career
step with a respected property. Skills: Exceptional communicator

"What in the world are you doing?"

Fox, from Apartment 19B, gazed up at me, using his hand as a visor to block the sun. "Yoga."

"Why are you wearing so many clothes?" He had on at least three sweat shirts, two beanies, mittens, and several pairs of sweat pants, like one of those padded guys who train police dogs to attack.

"I'm doing *hot* yoga." Fox pulled his right leg up and over his head. He was surprisingly flexible. I could barely touch my toes.

"Can you do this in your apartment and not in the middle of the courtyard where people are walking?" I asked.

"No way, man," he said on an exhale, eyes closed, forehead glistening. "My place is too hot for them."

"Them? Them who—*ouch*!" I looked down to see what had nipped the back of my leg. "What the heck? Where did this goat come from?"

"It's for me," Fox said. The small white goat trotted up on his back. "I'm doing hot goat yoga. Big audition Wednesday. I've got to get zen."

I wasn't sure how a barnyard animal on your back was supposed to help anyone *zen*. Not that it mattered because, "This is a no pet property...hold on. What is she eating? Is that...money?" I spun around. "Oh, come on!" My purse, which I had placed on the table two minutes ago, was now on the ground, the contents scattered. A small brown goat stood among the mess.

Oh, for the love of all that is unholy in this world!

The mom in me took over. I cupped my hand in front of the white goat's mouth. "Spit it out right now."

The goat listened about as well as my three-year-old did, and swallowed.

"Your goat ate all my money!" Really, he only ate a dollar. Until payday, that was all my money. "You need to— *ouch*!" The brown goat bit the back of my calf. *Sweet mother bleepin'!*

My name is Cambria Clyne. I'm an onsite apartment manager slash goat chew toy.

"You should try yoga. You need to chill," said Fox.

As much as I could use a good *chill*—especially after my disastrous New York trip—wearing eight layers of clothing with a money-eating animal on my back didn't sound like a good way to decompress.

That's what ice cream was for.

There were about five different house rules Fox was currently in violation of. Not that I had the time to run down each infraction. "We can talk about this incident later. Where is the cable guy?"

"Not sure." Fox lowered himself to the ground, looking as if he were about to do a push-up. The goat jumped down and screamed. I had no idea goats could scream. It sounded like a person had climbed inside the little creature and was crying for help. It was quite unpleasant.

"The cable company said they'd be here between twelve and five." Fox sat up, crossed his legs, and started to hum.

"Fox?"

He continued to hum while the goat continued to scream while I continued to curse under my breath and rub my sore calf.

Sometimes I really hate living in Los Angeles.

I shook Fox by the shoulders until his eyes opened. He stared up at me as if I'd just woken him from a deep sleep. If only I could shut my brain off so easily.

"Your message said the cable guy would be here at noon," I said.

"I didn't want to risk you missing him. I've been living with slow internet for *eight* days. And you've been too busy vacationing." He squeezed his eyes shut. "By the way, I saw you on TV."

My heart hiccupped. I did *not* want to think about New York. Not today. Not ever.

I checked my watch. It was almost three o'clock, and I had to leave soon if I was going to miss traffic.

From the thirteen messages Fox had left for me while I was away, I knew his internet was "inhumanely slow," and the cable company had to get into the attic in order to replace old wiring. The problem was, there were only four apartments that had access to the attic. I had to be there when the cable guy went in because all four units were occupied.

Wait a second.

Aha! Apartment 14B had attic access, and they'd moved out earlier in the morning. I hadn't had a chance to walk the apartment yet, but that shouldn't be a problem.

"Here's the deal," I said. "I have to be somewhere important in an hour. Apartment 14B moved out this morning, and I'll unlock the door. You can have the cable guy go through the attic in there. But he can't touch *anything* else." I grabbed my phone and sent a quick text to Mr. Nguyen, the maintenance supervisor, asking if he could swing by—*ouch!* "Stop biting me," I warned the little brown goat with a stern shake of my finger.

Note to self: Google what diseases goats carry.

Not that either one of them had broken the skin, but still. My hypochondriac mind had to know.

I finished my text and itched my nose using the backside of my hand. I was allergic to most things with fur, and goats were no exception.

Fox stood and rolled up his yoga mat. "I totally freaked when I saw you on TV. I was like '*dude, that's my apartment manager on* Celebrity Tango!'"

And we're back to that. Great.

I'd had two seconds of airtime during a quick scan of the audience on the season finale of *Celebrity Tango. Two seconds.* I'd already had a number of texts from friends, family, and residents saying they saw me. I'd underestimated how many people watched the show, and how recognizable my frizzy hair was.

"Bummer your friend didn't win," Fox said. "Third place isn't so bad."

"Not too bad," I agreed. Third place wasn't too bad at all, considering we thought she'd get kicked off during week one. However, according to Amy, third place was "the most horrid thing to ever happen" to her. I'd reminded her about that time she was framed for the murder of her costar, and she threw a golden stiletto at me. I guess *horrid* was subjective.

"How do you know Amy Montgomery?" Fox asked.

"We've been best friends since the third…grade." *Gulp.* I faltered when Fox began peeling off all his shirts, revealing a glistening six-pack. *Oh, my.* Yes, he's cocky, demanding, a royal thorn in my side, and I wouldn't shed a tear if he decided to move. He was also young and chiseled, and I was only a human being with eyeballs.

"I'd like to get on the show," he said. "Can you ask Amy for me?"

"I think you need to be a celebrity to be on *Celebrity Tango*."

"No problem. Have you seen my latest spread?"

"Are you talking about the STD billboard?"

"Yep."

"The one where you're crying?"

"Yep."

"The one along the 5 freeway?"

"Not just on the 5," he said. "That was a national campaign. It's also on the 405."

He must not have understood what *national* meant. "Congratulations—*ouch*!" The goat nipped at my calf. "Fox!"

"I know. I know. I know. I'll call the guy. I'm only renting them for the hour."

"You can rent a goat?"

"Sure. You can rent anything in Los Angeles."

"Good to know."

"By the way, why are you so fancy?"

"I'm not *that* fancy." I was wearing a blue Anthropology dress that matched my eyes and looked good against my pale, freckled skin. The dress was the most expensive thing in my closet, reserved for first dates and interviews only. Today was the latter.

Not that I could tell this to Fox.

I couldn't tell any of my residents.

Not until I was offered the job. Right now, I was the onsite property manager for a forty-unit apartment building in Los Angeles. I also managed a thirty-two-unit complex in Burbank. The building was close to Warner Bros. Studios, which meant most of my residents were varying degrees of starving actor. Actors who did things like hot yoga in the middle of the courtyard with little angry goats.

Note to self: Add no barnyard animals allowed on premises to house rules.

I went upstairs, unlocked Apartment 14B, and peeked inside to make sure there were no furniture or dead bodies left behind (you never knew in this business). The apartment was fairly clean, crime-free, and furniture-free. Perfect. I snapped a few pictures—specifically of the three years' worth of food crusted along the insides of the oven.

Move-outs would often scrub the entire apartment from floor to ceiling to toilet to bathtub, but forget to open the oven. A total bummer for all parties involved. For the resident, because I couldn't hire the cleaning company to come out for one thing. They charged me for the entire unit. A bummer for me because I had to deal with an irate former resident who was charged for cleaning when they spent hours doing it themselves.

Moral of the story?

Always check the oven.

I took one more picture with a date-stamp (should The Case of The Dirty Oven go to small claims court), then deemed the apartment safe for the cable company.

Down the stairs I went, through the courtyard, and past Fox. I managed to escape with only one new goat bite and made it to my car parked down the street. It was hot, and the smoggy air stung my lungs. I was looking forward to the end of summer. Mostly because I missed the cooler temperatures, but also because it meant the end of tourist season.

Speaking of tourists, I got stuck behind a double-decker bus coasting down California Street, going towards Warner Bros.

Studio. Passengers had their phones out, taking video and pictures of what? I had no idea. There was nothing but apartment buildings, a coffee shop, and a few palm trees along this road. All I knew for certain was they were going five miles per hour and I had someplace to be.

Once I was able to get on the freeway, traffic was surprisingly light. I arrived at Cedar Creek Apartments with ten minutes to spare. I rolled up to the curb and gripped the steering wheel, while peering up at the building.

You are doing the right thing, I reminded myself. *It's perfectly reasonable to want to advance in your career. You are doing the right thing.*

Still, it felt like I was being unfaithful. Like I was sneaking around, seeing other properties behind my boss's back. Which, I suppose, was exactly what I was doing. Patrick would not be happy when or if I quit, but he'd be exceptionally unhappy if I left to manage the property next door.

That's right. Cedar Creek was located *next* to the Los Angeles property where I both lived and managed. Roughly three million apartment complexes in the county, and I was asked to interview at the building twenty feet from my front door.

I parked around the corner, not wanting to risk one of my residents seeing my car in the carport and thinking I was in the office. Or seeing my car in front of Cedar Creek and come looking for me there.

I'd spent a significant amount of time overthinking this.

Cedar Creek Apartments was an imposing ten-story building with a gated wraparound parking lot and an underground parking structure. A cobblestoned walkway led up to a pair of whimsical wrought-iron doors. Brilliant red and yellow flowers were dispersed throughout the lavish landscaping. A koi pond glistened near the entrance, and trees towered like a fortress around the perimeter of the property, prohibiting guests from seeing the apartment building next door. A smart move by management. Cedar Creek looked like a Four Seasons, while my property looked more like a motel.

A well-managed motel, I might add.

I hurried down the sidewalk, keeping my bag close to my side, going through "selling points" in my head. *You should hire me because I'm driven, and passionate, and knowledgeable, and hard-working, and I have excellent—oomph.*

There was a step. A big step. A step painted red with a large, hard-to-miss sign warning pedestrians of the impending step. A step I always forgot was there until I was on my hands and knees and staring it.

Honest to goodness, Cambria. Get it together.

I dusted off my knees, rolled my shoulders, raised my head, and tried walking again. This time more successfully. I managed to make it to the front door without incident and rang the intercom. While I waited, I smoothed down my hair, which I'd nicknamed Einstein because it was dark and curly and had the I-just-rubbed-a-balloon-on-my-head look to it.

Mr. and Dr. Dashwood greeted me at the door, standing shoulder to shoulder, wearing manufactured smiles He had on a sweater vest and loafers. She had on pearls with a cardigan wrapped around her shoulders. They looked like the type of people who spent their nights having dinner at "the club."

"Welcome, Cambria." Dr. Dashwood made a sweeping gesture with her arm, and I stepped inside. The place smelled of honey and lavender with a hint of corporate air conditioning. The leasing office was to the right behind a glass wall with two mahogany desks on either side of the room. To the left was the lobby. The walls were beveled and painted a cream color with large abstract art hung every few feet. The coffee table was glass and positioned between two low-back couches. The place screamed sophistication, elegance, and money. Three words you'd use to describe the Dashwoods.

My three words would be *resourceful*, *clumsy*, and *hungry*.

Self-doubt began to worm its way into my thoughts. Could I manage a place like Cedar Creek? Could I *live* in a place like Cedar Creek? The lower-middle class were my people. Could I ditch my people for a fancy high-rise?

Then I saw the Wow Fridge near the hallway—basically a refrigerator filled with treats and drinks for residents to enjoy. And there was the Kids' Corner on the other side of the lobby—

basically a table with coloring books and crayons along with a small dollhouse. These little features felt more like *me*.

Food and crayons were basically my life right now.

"Please have a seat." Dr. Dashwood sat on the couch and crossed her ankles, resting her dainty hands in her lap. She had a diamond-studded bracelet dangling around her wrist and a wedding ring with a diamond roughly the size of China on her finger. My gosh. I had no idea how she lifted her hand with that thing on.

Mr. Dashwood plopped down beside his wife and stretched his legs out in front of him. He already looked bored.

I hugged my purse and slid onto the couch opposite them. The coffee table between us appeared to be a mile long, and I could feel myself shrink a little.

"I was so happy when you called," Dr. Dashwood said. "We were worried you wouldn't interview."

"I was hesitant at first, only because I didn't want to quit my current job less than a year in." Also, I wasn't sure I even wanted to continue in property management. I'd already been cursed at, yelled at, shot at, actually shot, taken hostage, arrested, and now bitten by a goat. But Cedar Creek came with a big pay raise, and if there was one thing I'd learned from my New York trip, it was that I needed funds in reserve at all times because I was a terrible decision maker. Legal documents were expensive. Also, Lilly was starting school tomorrow, and preschool was basically the same price as a college education. "After careful consideration," I said, trying to sound more confident, "I believe this would be an excellent step in my career, and I know I'd do a good job."

"I'm happy to hear it. Truth is, I thought we'd spend at least a month here, but we're ready to get back to Arizona and resume our normal lives. What we need is a manager who can function without constant supervision, and provide us with daily rundowns of what is happening. As you can imagine, we've been on damage control since the *incident*."

By *incident* she meant the last manager was killed. I could understand why she wouldn't want to mention the murder of the previous manager to the potential new manager. Could put a damper on the interviewing process.

"Shall we get started?" Dr. Dashwood sat up a little straighter, so I did, too.

"Absolutely." My phone dinged from inside of my purse. *Oops.* "I'm so sorry. Incoming text message." I reached in and silenced my cell without checking it first. Whoever it was, they could wait.

Dr. Dashwood launched into a series of questions regarding my previous employment, current employment, and about my knowledge of their management software system. Much to my surprise, I was killing it. Typically, interviews turned me into a sweaty mess, and I'd fumble over my words, swallow excessively, blurt out embarrassing TMI details, and start every sentence with "um."

Not today.

Today I was Confident Cambria! I knew my craft, and I'd seen just about everything you could think of since becoming an apartment manager, from skinny dippers at midnight to dead bodies in the dumpster. So when Dr. Dashwood asked me how I might handle a resident who was playing his music too loud, I could easily answer with, "I'd ask them once to turn it down. The second warning would be written in a formal complaint. The third would come with a Notice to Quit."

The only problem was my freaking phone would not stop. It continued to pulse in my purse every few minutes, alerting me of an incoming text message. My daughter, Lilly, was with her dad. If it were an emergency, he'd call not text. If there were a problem at either of the properties I managed, I'd get a call on the emergency line. No one texts urgent information.

I placed my purse on the floor and continued the interview.

Dr. Dashwood spent the next thirty minutes going over the property specifics: the sauna, the pool, the spa, the gym, the theater room, the game room, the conference room, and all the other rooms that made up the massive apartment building.

Mr. Dashwood didn't utter a single word. Instead, he sat there with the face of a man who was trying *really* hard not to fall asleep.

"Then, of course, we have the manager's apartment located on the second floor," Dr. Dashwood said. "It's a two bedroom, two bath, and you'd receive a discount rent. I understand you have a daughter."

"Yes, her name is Lilly and she's three." *And she'll put her handprints all over those beautiful glass walls.*

Dr. Dashwood smiled. You could tell her teeth were capped and expensive. "Do you have your résumé?"

"It's right here in my bag…" Oh no. The folder that held my freshly printed résumé was missing an entire side, and the crisp 8 ½ by 11, 100% cotton, white paper was gone.

Stupid goat.

I sat there, bent over, with my hand in my bag, flustered, my heart racing while every pore on my body began to pump out sweat at hyper speed. Crap.

Crap. *Crap.* Crap!

As I saw it, I had three options. I could one: tell them the truth. Say a goat ate my résumé. Then proceed to spend twenty minutes overexplaining how this had happened. I could two: say I'd email it to her. Or, I could three: continue to sit there in a sweaty, speechless mess.

Number three was tempting, but two felt more professional. "I'm so sorry. I don't have my résumé on me right now. I'd be happy to email it as soon as we're done."

The Dashwoods exchanged a look, a flash of disappointment on their faces. Dang it!

This interview just took a nosedive.

My stomach went all slithery, and I fought the urge to overexplain myself—a bad habit of mine.

"Go ahead and email it to me," Dr. Dashwood said. "Let's have a tour. Shall we?"

"Yes, *please*," Mr. Dashwood said, joining the conversation.

Dr. Dashwood led the way, taking us down a long hall. The walls were beveled and cream, and the sconces were brass. I listened to the click of her heels on the marble flooring until she stopped at the elevator. "We'll start on the tenth floor." She pressed the button, and I could hear the hum of the motor from the utility closet.

I really, really hated elevators.

While we waited for the doors to part, I stole a quick glance at my phone. I had eleven text messages from Fox.

Fox: Cable guy is here, but Mr. Nguyen isn't. Can he go in?

Fox: ?

Fox: ?

Fox: U there?

Fox: Cable dude went into the apartment. He's in the attic.

Fox: He accidentally knocked down a wall.

Fox: Can he move the drum behind the wall?

Fox: ?

Fox: ?

Fox: He can't get to the cables unless he moves the drum.

Fox: U there?

"Cambria?"

I gazed up at Dr. Dashwood. "Yes?" I asked.

"I said would you rather start with the amenities? Or do you need to take care of personal business?"

"Oh, no, no. This isn't personal." I forced a laugh, which sounded an awful lot like a Miss Piggy impression. "It's a resident who is texting me. He's having trouble with his cable, and they're there in the attic and... It can wait." I dropped my phone into my bag. "The amenities would be wonderful." I flashed a smile.

"Very well. They're located on the first floor. Right this way." Dr. Dashwood continued down the hallway, talking about how they'd purchased the building years ago with the idea of turning it into one of Los Angeles's top luxury apartments. She pointed to the art and the rugs and told me she'd worked with a designer to come up with the classic theme. I oohed and ahhed and nodded along until she turned her back and I could text Fox back.

Me: How did he accidentally knock down a wall?

Fox: It was really just some wood taped together.

Me: And there is a drum?

Fox: The one in the attic behind the wall in the corner. Can he move it?

Fox: Never mind. He said he can't move furniture. Can I move it?

I had absolutely *no* idea what he was talking about.

Me: Please don't touch anything until Mr. Nguyen gets there.

"What do you think, Cambria?" asked Dr. Dashwood.

I hid my phone behind my back and spun around. "Wonderful," I said, even though I had absolutely *no* idea what we were talking about.

"So you like the idea?"

Dr. Dashwood looked so excited that I couldn't help but answer, "Of course," with as much enthusiasm as I could muster.

"See, dear?" Dr. Dashwood placed a dainty hand on her husband's shoulder. "He didn't believe any manager would agree to take on the task, but I knew you would. Residents will love the variety. And no other community in the area is doing it."

Oh no, what did I just say was a good idea?

My phone buzzed. I ached to read the message, but Dr. Dashwood was still talking to me. "Let's continue our tour," she said, and we spent the next twenty minutes walking through each of the many amenities Cedar Creek offered. The pool was so blue it almost hurt my eyes. The theater room looked like…well, a movie theater. The gym looked like a 24 Hour Fitness. When we moved to the underground parking garage, I began to realize how much work managing this place would be. Yikes. I'd need an excellent assistant manager and an even better maintenance crew.

Speaking of which.

"What about the rest of the staff?" I asked. When they'd asked if I'd interview for the position, there was talk of allowing me to hire the maintenance supervisor and assistant—should I get the job, of course.

As if on cue, a golf cart zoomed by with *Cedar Creek Maintenance* painted on the side. The cart stopped in front of a utility closet, and a tall man with a ponytail of brown hair grabbed a tool bag from the front seat.

"That's Stan," Dr. Dashwood said. "We were simply *desperate* for a new maintenance supervisor, and he was able to start right away. As you can imagine, this place requires constant work to maintain its elegance."

Oh. OK.

"We will have our new manager interview assistant managers," she added as an afterthought. "It's important that everyone work as a well-oiled, crime-free machine."

Couldn't argue with that.

"Of course, we are still interviewing candidates for the management position," Dr. Dashwood continued. "It's vital that our new manager be honest, hard-working, and not be involved in scandal of any kind. The news has *finally* died down since the *incident*. We don't want Cedar Creek's name in the papers ever again, unless it's to talk about the beautiful ambiance and high-class living quarters."

"Of course," I said, wondering if she'd heard about the three murder investigations I'd been involved in. One had been her previous manager. I was actually shot on the premises. If she had chosen to forget the shooting, fine by me.

That was the old Cambria, anyway. The new Cambria didn't get herself involved in criminal cases. I mean, what were the odds I'd happen upon a dead body again?

My phone buzzed.

"You are on the top of our list," Dr. Dashwood said. "Should we hire you, how much of a notice would you need to give next door?"

"My contract says thirty days, but I'd like to give my boss enough time to find someone new if I took the job."

"*If.*" Dr. Dashwood grasped her pearls. "Do you have other offers? Because we have excellent benefits." She snapped her fingers.

That must have been Mr. Dashwood's cue to speak. "We offer medical, dental, and vision. You'll receive monthly bonuses, a discounted apartment, and reimbursement for your cell phone."

I almost passed out. I'd known it would be more money (*a lot* more money). But monthly bonuses? Plus vision! My eyes were fine, as far as I knew. I'd never been to an optometrist. But only because I didn't have vision insurance. Maybe I was clumsy because I needed glasses.

OK, I really want this job.

Not that money was everything.

But you can't put a price on vision.

"We'll be doing a full background and credit check on you," Mr. Dashwood said. "And we'll need to speak to your previous and current employers."

The thought of them calling Patrick made me nauseated.

"Is that a problem?" Dr. Dashwood asked.

"No, it's only that I haven't told my boss that you asked me to interview here." My phone buzzed. Oh, for heaven's sakes! "Can I just…um…use the restroom?"

"Absolutely. It's upstairs. I'll show you."

"I know where it is," I said and hurried up the stairs. Last month, when the previous manager went missing, I'd spent quite a bit of time there. It's part of the reason the Dashwoods asked me to interview. They were impressed with how I'd stepped in to help without asking for pay. I'd also unraveled a massive scandal involving inflated rents, secret accounts, and a convoluted gambling scheme—really, why wouldn't they hire me? I was basically a detective with an expertise in Fair Housing laws.

The bathroom was down the hall, near the maintenance office. I pushed open the door and took a seat on the toilet. I had six new text messages from Fox.

He'd sent me a picture of the drum. In my head, the drum was a *drum*, as in a percussion. My head was wrong. This was a drum you'd store water or grains in. It was metal, dirty, covered in webs, and I'd call it a barrel not a drum.

Fox: I'm going to move it.

Fox: U there?

Fox: It's really heavy.

Fox: What's in this thing?

Fox: Can I take the lid off?

Fox: U there?

I had no idea what was in the barrel or where it came from, but it looked like it had been there a long time.

Me: Please don't touch anything until Mr. Nguyen gets there.

Fox: Can I pry open the lid with a crowbar?

Me: Please, please don't touch anything with a crowbar.

I composed a separate text to Mr. Nguyen, asking for his ETA, when there was a knock on the door.

"Cambria? Are you all right in there?" Dr. Dashwood asked.

"I'm perfectly well," I said in an awkward, high-pitched voice. "I'll be out shortly."

Mr. Nguyen texted back: *I'm ten minutes out.*

Perfect!

Me: Mr. Nguyen will be there in ten minutes. Don't touch anything.

Fox: Too late. I opened the lid, but it looks like someone is in there.

Me: You mean something?

Fox: SomeONE.

Me: As in a person?

Fox: A dead person. A really, really dead person.

Me: Are you sure?

Fox sent me a picture he took looking down on the barrel. The photo was dark and out of focus. I was able to vaguely make out the top of a human head with dark hair.

Guess I was wrong. Turned out there *were* people who delivered urgent news via text.

CHAPTER TWO

Can easily handle the deadly and unexpected.

I told the Dashwoods there was a resident in desperate need of my help, and they encouraged me to go. I may not have mentioned the resident in need was dead, but they didn't ask. Instead, Dr. Dashwood said, "I'm impressed with your dedication, even on your day off."

She'd obviously not spent much time as a property manager. Otherwise she'd know there was no such thing as a day off.

I raced back to the Burbank building, double parked my car at the curb, smacked on the hazard lights, and crawled over the center console—the driver's side door was stuck shut, and had been since an incident with a runaway dumpster.

There were no emergency vehicles or police activity of any kind. It wouldn't have surprised me if Fox had thought to text me before calling 9-1-1. He wasn't exactly the sharpest tool in the shed.

Which got me thinking.

What if the person in the drum was a prop? We were close to all the studios. A former resident could have stored a realistic corpse made of plastic in the attic years ago and forgotten about it. Seemed unlikely Fox would confuse a *really, really dead person* with a *really, really fake one*. But a girl can dream.

Oh, please, please, please let it be a prop. Please, please, please.

I found Fox in the courtyard, huddled near the stairwell with a gray-haired man wearing a cable company shirt.

"Are you sure it's an actual person in the barrel and not a prop?" I asked in lieu of a hello. There was no time for pleasantries.

The grim expressions plastered on the two men's faces answered my questions. Crap.

"Cambria?" came a voice from above. I looked up. Mr. Nguyen was leaning over the railing.

"Oh good, you're here." I felt a whoosh of relief. Mr. Nguyen was the most reasonable and trustworthy person I knew. "What's going on?"

"There's a barrel in the attic, and inside is a dead person. Looks like it's been there for a long time."

I slapped my hand over my mouth. Why-oh-why-oh-*whhhyyy* does this keep happening? Am I stuck in some sort of purgatory? Is this what happens when you spend your free time watching crime shows? Life begins to imitate art?

Note to self: Start watching The Bachelorette.

Then instead of dead people popping up every freaking day, I'd have twenty men arriving in limos, vying for my affection, wanting to marry me—actually, scratch that. The premise hit a little too close to home. I should give up television altogether just to be on the safe side.

"I can't unsee what I saw." Fox screwed his fists into his eye sockets. "Totally ruined my Zen."

"Me, too." The cable guy pulled a package of cigarettes from his front shirt pocket.

"This is a no smoking property," I said.

"Lady, I just found a dead body." He placed the cigarette between his lips. "My nerves are shot."

Yours and mine both, buddy. "I'm sorry for—*ouch!* What the...Fox, why is there a goat still here?"

"It's possible I misread the ad and I accidentally bought them."

"How do you accidentally buy two goats?"

"I don't know, man. My brain is still tripping because of the dead person in the attic!"

Marlene from Apartment 11A, who was casually walking by, paused midstep. She had grocery bags in her arms and concern all over her face.

I smiled my best everything-is-fine-and-everyone-is-alive smile and waved. "Have a great day."

Marlene wasn't buying it. "What happened—*ouch!*" The little brown goat head-butted her leg and chased her away before she could finish her thought. Marlene squealed and slammed the door to her apartment.

Palm, meet forehead.

"Please control the goats," I said to Fox, keeping my voice low. "Did you call the police?"

He stared at me, as if the thought of calling the LAPD to inform them of the dead body had not crossed his mind.

"Right. OK. Just…relax here, and I'll see what's going on." I went up the stairs, my hand gliding along the railing as I took each step. I could not believe Fox hadn't called the police. Then again, everyone handles stressful situations differently. For example, I obsessively ate.

Speaking of which, I could have really used a gallon of mint chip right about then.

Mr. Nguyen was in Apartment 14B, standing in the middle of the room with his phone pressed to his ear, speaking in Vietnamese. When he saw me hovering in the doorway, he covered the receiver and mouthed, *I already called the police.*

Thank you, I mouthed back and stepped inside the studio apartment.

The attic access was really just a square hole in the stucco ceiling. A ladder was set up below, presumably from the cable guy, because it didn't look like Mr. Nguyen's. Also, it said property of the cable company on the side.

As previously mentioned, I was basically a detective.

A part of me wanted to walk away, put as much distance between me and whatever heinous crime had happened there. But the more logical part of my brain (or maybe it was the more illogical part—it had become harder and harder to distinguish between the two) told me to stay. I climbed up the ladder and peeked into the attic. I'd never been up there before, mostly because there wasn't a reason to. As far as I knew, it was nothing but beams, insulation, and wires.

And guess what?

It was nothing but beams, insulation, and wires. No barrel. At least, not one that I could see.

I crawled up and in, minding the space so I wouldn't hit my head. The ceiling was low, and the flooring was mostly exposed insulation. I walked along a beam, keeping one hand on the wall for support. Around the corner was more attic, more beams, and more insulation. I kept going, maintaining my balance, which did not come naturally to me. I was quite proud of myself...*umpph.*

Never mind.

My foot landed in the pink fluffy stuffing, and it felt like I'd just shoved my leg into a bath of needles. Holy crap!

Note to self: Have Mr. Nguyen cover floors with wood. Ouch!

This was precisely why I typically wore jeans to work. Between the goat and the insulation, my poor legs would never be the same.

I scratched my calf and continued walking. The building was in a U-shape, and I turned the last corner and found a finished floor and the barrel. Metal, dusty, and so innocuous it practically blended in with the wall. Which is probably why it stood there untouched for as long as it did. The lid was off, and the smell permeating the air was quite pungent. I did not want to subject my eyeballs to what was inside. Fox's blurry picture was enough. All I knew for sure was there was no way someone was able to carry a barrel filled with a human up a ladder and across the unfinished attic floor. The murder either happened up here, or perhaps in one of the units on this side of the building, and the killer stashed the body right above their apartment. Kind of creepy. But I'd learned during my short stint in property management that people are, in general, kind of creepy.

I did a quick search to make sure there were no other barrels, bins, or boxes large enough to store a human. All I found was a step stool, two large pieces of plywood that looked to have worked as a makeshift wall around the barrel, and a timeworn pillow with frayed seams. No bodies. Thank goodness.

I walked across the beam, back to Apartment 14B, and climbed down. Mr. Nguyen hadn't moved. His phone was in his hands, fingers flying across the screen. "The police should be here any minute," he said without looking up. "And I called Chase."

"Chase!" I slipped down the last two steps of the ladder. "Why did you call Chase?"

"Isn't that what we do when you find a dead body?"

I stood up straight and swiped a strand of Einstein from my forehead. "To be fair, I didn't find the dead body. Fox did."

"Did you want me to call Chase back and tell him not to come?"

"No, I guess not." Detective Chase Cruller (like the donut) was a little older than me. Early thirties. Dark blond hair. Five o'clock shadow no matter the time of day. Green eyes. Superhuman good looks. And he was pretty much my boyfriend. At least he *was*.

Our relationship title was currently under advisement.

"Why do you look so fancy?" Mr. Nguyen gave me the once-over with a confused tilt of his head.

"I had a…a…a…an interview. " I couldn't lie to him. I loved Mr. Nguyen. He was family. You don't lie to family. Unless that family are your parents. Then you tell little white lies to keep them from having massive anxiety attacks and/or collapsing in a puddle of disappointment over the fact their only child is a complete and total mess.

Mr. Nguyen didn't hide the shock from his face. "Did you interview at Cedar Creek?"

"Yes," I said, not wanting to look him in the eye. I'd been the one who got him the job with Elder Property Management. We worked great together. Leaving him would be hard.

"I thought you were not going to interview there."

"I had a change of heart and decided to go for it." I massaged my temples, feeling a tension headache coming on. "I doubt I'll get the job now. Not after this debacle."

"Why? You didn't kill the person."

"No, but after what happened with their last manager, they're wanting to bring on someone new who doesn't have baggage. I'd say finding a dead body in the attic is baggage."

"How will they know?"

True. "How *would* they know?" I tapped my chin. "It's not like this will make the news. I mean, this is Los Angeles. There are dead bodies all over the place, right?"

"Not all over the place. Just wherever you are."

He was right. The Dashwoods didn't need to know about any of the other murders I'd happened upon, including the body in the attic. *Pfft.* There was nothing to worry about.

Correction: there was everything to worry about, but sometimes (like two or three times a year) I tried to be optimistic.

* * *

The police arrived, followed by a CSI van and several unmarked police cars. A crime scene investigator pulled yellow tape in front of Apartment 14B's door, while a detective interviewed Fox and the cable guy, who was standing outside by the curb, smoking, because I wouldn't allow him to light up in the courtyard.

House rules are house rules, whether there was a decomposing body on the premise or not.

Turned out the old cable wiring ran under a wall in the attic, and when the cable guy had yanked hard on the cable, the wall had fallen down. That's when he'd discovered the wall was nothing but two pieces of plywood held together with a few nails, glue, and duct tape. The barrel was inside, and per company rules, the cable guy could not move it. So Fox did, thus the discovery of the dead body.

Now the place was buzzing with police officers coming to and from the attic. I stood in the doorway of my office, watching, fretting, and biting at my bottom lip until I saw him. *Chase.* He walked past the mailboxes and into the courtyard. His hips deliciously swayed as if someone had pushed *slow-mo*, and he took off his sunglasses, revealing the bandage keeping his right eyebrow together.

I stood up straighter and smoothed out the front of my dress, picking off a few bits of lint clinging to the linen.

Chase bypassed the officers gathered in the courtyard and came straight to me. "How are you doing?"

"Wonderful!" I said. Stupid choice of wording, considering the situation.

"I'm glad to hear it." Chase cupped my cheek in his hand, and I resisted the urge to throw my arms around his neck, drag him inside, and swing the door closed.

Instead, I sneezed.

Chase dropped his hand. "Why are you so dressed up?"

"I made a last minute decision to interview at Cedar Creek."

"Good for you." His eyes slid down. "Why do you have a goat?"

"Because if I put her down, she bites the back of my leg."

Chase shook his head. "I swear if I had your job, I'd be a raging alcoholic."

"It's a good thing I cope with ice cream."

"Yes, it is." He winked his uninjured eye. "When are we going to finish talking about the trip?"

"Soon," I promised. But I was carrying a goat, and there was a dead person in the attic, and I was really good at avoiding subjects I didn't want to talk about. "But first, do we know anything about this person who was in the barrel?"

"I do." Hampton sauntered over, hiking up his pants. Hampton was Chase's partner. He wore a horrible toupee that looked like a squirrel had crawled on top of his head and died. Also, he wore his pants really high. Like really, *really*, wedgie-in-the-front-and-back high. "Initial inspections tell us the victim was female, dark hair, with a petite frame. We're taking the barrel down to the medical examiner to see if we can identify her with dental records."

"How long has she been there?"

"My guess would be somewhere between twenty and thirty years."

A hollow space formed in the pit of my stomach. This poor woman had been shoved in a barrel for three decades. Now that's *horrid*.

"If we can't find the identity, we'll give word to local news stations that a body has been discovered, give a description and time frame, and see what leads that brings," Hampton said. "Be prepared. There will be media around here."

"No! That's a terrible idea," I blurted out. "You can't let the public know. It's…it's…inhumane."

"How is that inhumane?" Chase asked.

"I don't know! But please, please, don't tell the press."

"Why don't you want this made public?' Hampton asked.

So my potential new boss doesn't find out.

Not that I could admit this out loud. I felt selfish enough for even thinking it. Truth was, how could I deny the victim her chance for justice?

"It's fine," I finally said. "You do whatever it is that you need to do."

"Good. And why do you have a goat?" Hampton asked.

"Long story." I paused to sneeze and scratch the backside of my calf. "I'd really like to keep this apartment building out of the press, though. Do you have any idea when you're going to release the information?"

"We'll wait to see what the medical examiner is able to uncover," Hampton said. "I doubt this will stay quiet for long, though." He pointed up, and I followed his gaze. Fox was taking a selfie in front of the crime scene tape.

Oh, great.

I marched up the stairs, still holding the goat. She was much more compliant when she wasn't roaming free. "You can't post anything about this online," I said to Fox.

"Why not? I'm the one who found the dead body." He held up his phone and flashed a peace sign. "Say cheese."

"Wait, wait, wait. I don't want to be in *any* pictures."

"Why not? You're dressed nice today. Might as well."

"Here's the deal…um… This is official police business. Posting anything on social media could…hurt the case. You wouldn't want that, would you?"

"What am I supposed to do, then?" he asked.

"What do you mean?"

"Do I just not, like, post anything about this?"

"*Yes.*"

Fox appeared confused. "So just not post anything."

"Yes."

"Nothing?"

"Nothing."

Silence fell while Fox's eyes went from his phone, then to me, then to the goat, then back to his phone. He did this several times. "For how long?"

"Ever."

"Wow. That's a long time."

"It is," I agreed, trying to sound supportive.

"I think I could do that," he said with slow determination. "Like a social media cleanse."

"Even better. Now, let's get out of the way." I escorted him down the stairs and thrust the goat into his arms. "And please return the goats. This is a no pet property. It will cause a lot of problems with your neighbors." Two days ago, Apartment 3A had asked if they could have a teacup Pomeranian, and I'd said no. I could only imagine how upset they'd be if they thought I said no to a two-pound dog and yes to two thirty-pound goats.

I went back to my office—and by office, I mean a storage closet with a desk. Chase was sitting in a metal folding chair waiting for me.

"Are you not working this case?" I asked him.

"Hampton and I are on it."

"Any word from the FBI while I was gone?" Chase had applied, been approved, and was now awaiting orders. I knew he was anxious to find out when he'd be sent off for training, and even more anxious about what would happen between us while he was gone.

"No news yet," he said.

I yanked open the old filing cabinet and started searching through the files.

"Cambria, what are you doing?"

"There are only four apartments with attic access. Chances are whoever killed this poor woman lived in one of those. The barrel was all the way to the right side of the building and hidden behind two pieces of plywood in a corner. So I'm thinking it was Apartment 2B or 4B."

"I doubt it was anyone who has lived here within the last twenty years. Do you have files that go back that far?"

"No, I only have the current and previous occupants of each unit. But it's a start. There are a few longtime residents." I pulled out the folders for Apartments 14B, 12B, 4B, and 2B. "I'll ask Patrick for the archived files. Are you going to tell him about this, or should I?" I dreaded having to tell my boss we had another murder.

"Hampton is going to talk to him."

"What about the McMillses?"

"I'm going to talk to them." The McMillses owned both the Burbank and Los Angeles buildings along with several other properties up and down the California coast. They were old and rich and not involved. Their nephew, Trevor, managed the McMills Trust, while Patrick's management company oversaw the residential properties. In short, I was pretty far down the totem pole.

"How long before we get information from the medical examiner?" I asked.

"Anywhere from twenty-four hours to six weeks, depending on the preliminary findings."

"That's a massive time frame."

"You don't need to worry. We're good at our job. We'll find out what happened."

"I'm not doubting your *detectiveness*. But it can't hurt to have someone like me digging around."

"Actually, it could." He pried a file from my grasp and set it on the desk. "I want you to leave it to us, but I understand that's an impossible request for you. All I'm going to say is *be careful*."

"Aren't I always?"

"No, you're never careful. You are the least careful person I know. You are the exact opposite of careful. You can be downright reckless."

"OK. OK." Geez. "Tell me how you really feel."

"I did tell you, and I ended up with this." He pointed to the butterfly bandage on his eyebrow.

"We don't need to get into that right now." Or ever. "I promise to be careful and report back any of my findings." I crossed my heart.

Chase regarded me under an intense gaze, and my knees went a bit wobbly. He had that effect on me. "Is the reason you don't want this out in the public because if the Dashwoods find out, they might not offer you the job?"

"Maybe."

"So that's a yes. I can read you pretty well, Cambria."

"Oh, really?" I grabbed hold of his tie and pulled him closer. "What am I thinking right now?"

Chase snaked his arm around my waist. His scent was intoxicating, and my legs turned to goo. He brushed his lips along my jawline until his mouth was at my ear. I sucked in a shaky breath, forgetting my troubles for only a moment.

"Not until we have *the* conversation," he whispered.

Ah, crud.

Chase released me from his arms, and I had to use the edge of the desk to keep upright.

"Remember what I said. Be careful." He put his sunglasses on, ran a hand through his hair, and left.

Oh, my.

CHAPTER THREE

Proficient in the art of self-defense

I was back at the Los Angeles property by six o'clock. It felt good to be home. Sure, the place wasn't a sparkling high-rise with glass walls like next door. It was a two-story stucco building with brown fascia, brownish-greenish grass, three courtyards separated by ivy-laced breezeways, and apartments that weren't numbered in order, but I loved living there. Mostly.

The carports were bustling with residents who had arrived home from a long day at work, and I scratched the back of my calf as I walked into the first courtyard. Larry, from Apartment 32, stopped me to talk about his latest health crises (kidney stones, a mysterious rash on his heinie, upcoming surgery on his legs, hay fever, and hemorrhoids). I waived to Julie from Apartment 5. Then Daniella from Apartment 13 confronted me near the bushes to loudly express her outrage over the fact I wouldn't allow her to keep her hairless cat. I told her the answer was still: "This is a no pet property." I should have just tattooed the phrase on my forehead because I said it so much. Daniella expressed her outrage in both English and Spanish and stormed off.

I went straight to the mailboxes and dug around in my bag, searching for the keys, and located them under a container of fish crackers.

"Apartment manager!" came a familiar voice, and I willed myself invisible. "Apartment manager!"

I pulled out my mail, which consisted of bills and credit card offers, and slammed the little metal door. "Hi, Silvia. What can I do for you?"

Silvia Kravitz looked like the seventy-year-old love child of Gollum and Joan Rivers, thanks to about ten too many facelifts. She only wore lingerie, no matter the time of day (or position of the sun), and her pet parrot, Harold, could be found perched on her shoulder at all times. I'd dubbed her the mayor of Rumorville. She had something to say about everyone at all times. Even though her overbearing demeanor had calmed slightly over the past few weeks (thanks to a new love interest, aka Hampton), she still managed to find something to complain about daily.

"Do you eat Chinese?" she asked.

"Huh?"

"Do. You. Eat. Chinese. *Food*?"

"I like Chinese food," I said, scared where this conversation was going. "If that's what you're asking."

"What about Italian?" she asked.

Harold turned his backside to me. I wasn't sure what I ever did to that parrot, but I knew he didn't like me. I could feel him judging me with his little black beady eyes. That is, when he would *actually* look at me.

"I'm a fan of all food. *Why* do you ask?"

"Hampton and I want to double date."

Ahhhh!

"I told the boys I'd set it up."

Ahhhh!

"What! You talked to Chase about this?" I didn't mean to shout, but there's no way Chase would agree to a double date.

Unless this was payback for what happened during my trip. Except Chase was a cop. He'd made an oath to "always uphold the Constitution," and a night out with Silvia Kravitz would be considered cruel and unusual punishment.

"Yes," Silvia said. "We are available on Friday night. See you then."

"I-I-I-I-I-I…" I was still stammering when Silvia walked away, her silk robe flapping in the wind behind her while I stood there like a statue carved of mortified flesh. "I-I-I…no." *No. No. No. No!* I fumbled my phone out of my bag. Chase knew how I felt about Silvia. The woman had criticized me since I started working there. She even started a rumor on an apartment review website that I'd had a threesome with the retired couple in Apartment 22! Sure, the review was eventually deleted. Not before it had been seen by thousands of potential (and current) tenants. I was still getting messages from nursing home residents asking if I had vacancies.

This was *horrid*!

I sent Chase a text.

Me: Did you OK a date with Hampton and Silvia?

Three dots danced in the corner of my screen while he typed his response.

…Still waiting…

It couldn't possibly take that long to write *no*.

…Still waiting…

"Mommy!" Lilly called my name, and I looked up from my phone. She cut across the courtyard grass. "Mommy!"

I bent my knees and braced for impact. Lilly jumped into my arms, and I kissed the tip of her nose. "Hey there, kiddo. What are you doing here? I thought you were with Daddy."

"He dropped her off." Mrs. Nguyen ran up, her forehead glistening and her breath labored. "You need to wait for me," she said to Lilly. "I getting too old."

"Are you OK? Do you need to sit down?" I put Lilly on the ground. "Should I get a chair?"

"Stop your fussing. I'm not dying." She gave me the once-over. "Why are you so fancy?"

"I had an interview. Patrick doesn't know."

"You decided to do the job next door? Why?"

"It's an excellent opportunity for me and Lilly. I'm so sorry."

"Don't apologize to me. This is good. But Mr. Nguyen told me about your newest dead body. What did the Cedar Creek owners say about that?"

"They don't know, and, for the record, it's not *my* dead body. A resident found her. I wasn't even on the property."

"You're cursed."

"You are probably right." I grabbed Lilly's hand and started towards my apartment. Mrs. Nguyen walked with us. "Where's Tom?" I asked.

"He said something came up with work, and he dropped Lilly with me. He looked terrible. Awful. What happened to his arm?"

"It's a *long*, complicated story." As were most stories involving my one-night-stand-turned-baby-daddy. Thomas "Tom" Dryer (as in the appliance) was a defense attorney who represented the poor and falsely accused. He too had superhuman good looks. Was tall. Very tall. Dark hair. Hazel eyes. Looked like a young Dylan McDermott, if you squinted and tilted your head to the side. My parents thought he was gay, but he'd slept with just about every woman in the United States of America, so I knew he wasn't.

"Your life is a mess," Mrs. Nguyen said.

Ain't that the truth. "I'm sorry Tom dropped her here. He never even sent me a text." I checked my phone to be sure. Nothing from Tom *or* Chase.

"You don't need to say sorry. What you need to do is get your life figured out."

"I'm working on it."

"Work harder." We stopped at my door, and Mrs. Nguyen tucked a loose curl behind Lilly's ear. "Be good," she said, and the two conversed in Vietnamese while I waited. I loved that Lilly was fluent in two languages at the age of three. I was barely fluent in one language at the age of twenty-nine.

We said good-bye to Mrs. Nguyen and watched her walk to her apartment in the back of the building.

"When did Daddy drop you off here?" I asked Lilly.

"Forever ago."

That could be anywhere from ten minutes to an hour in toddler time. "Sorry I wasn't home. Let's make dinner, and we can…" I shoved the key into the lock of my apartment, and the door pushed open. *Weird?* I peeked my head in. "Hello? Anyone here?" I had locked the door and set the alarm that morning. I was sure of it. I'd found myself on the wrong end of a gun enough times to know the importance of home security. "Hello!" I called out again.

The keypad for the alarm was visible from the front door, and the light was green, signaling the alarm for my apartment was off.

"Stay here," I told Lilly and dug my pepper spray out of my bag. The lid had been chewed, rendering the spray completely useless. Damn goat!

At least it would make a good prop.

Unless my intruder had a gun.

Then it wouldn't be a good prop at all.

I had my phone in one hand, and the pepper spray-less in the other, and tiptoed into the living room. My apartment was a two bed, two bath, with a square kitchen that had a counter overlooking a dining area. A hallway led to the bedrooms and bathrooms, and the main living space was spacious with enough room for a couch and television.

"Oh, my gosh," I said under my breath. I'd left a bowl coated with ice cream on the TV stand this morning, and it was gone. Lilly's pajamas were folded nicely and sitting in a laundry basket instead of in a pile on the floor. I checked the kitchen. All my dishes were done, by *hand*, and sitting in a drying rack on the counter. The pizza box I'd crammed into the trash can was gone. The appliances had been wiped down and the floor swept.

I dialed 9-1-1 and opened the door to the office. The alarm sounded off, and I typed in the code. My office and the attached lobby were my favorite part of the property. I'd designed them myself (after I'd burned the place down, but whatever). The furniture was sleek, the art abstract. There were two palms by the door, and we had a vibrant orange accent wall. My desk was bamboo and littered with papers and random keys, the shredder was full, and the counter overlooking the lobby had a thin layer of dust.

The dispatch operator answered on the third ring. "Nine-one-one. What is your emergency?"

"Yes, someone broke into my apartment, and they…cleaned it."

"Someone broke into your apartment, and they…cleaned it?" the operator repeated, her voice monotone. I could almost hear her rolling her eyes.

"*Yes.*" I twisted open the blinds in my apartment. "The windows are even clean."

"Are you sure this was a break-in?"

"I mean"— I did a full spin—"nothing is broken."

Lilly pushed the front door open. "Can me come inside now?"

"It's *I*, and no. Wait right there." With my pepper spray in hand, and a dispatch operator who likely thought I was nuts in my ear, I walked down the hall. My bedroom door was cracked open, and I could hear the faintest sound of movement. "I called the police!" I kicked open the door and screamed.

"Ma'am, are you there?" the operator asked.

I clutched my chest. "Yes, I'm… It was a misunderstanding. Sorry." I hung up and tossed my phone at Amy, who was lying on my bed with AirPods on and a giant stuffed elephant beside her.

"Oh, hey!" Amy plucked a pod from her ear. "What's with the pepper spray?"

"I thought someone broke in." I leaned into the hallway. "Lilly, you can come inside! It's only Auntie Amy!"

"*Only*. Gosh. What a reception." Amy swung her legs over the side of the bed. "By the way, your place was a mess."

"I was in a hurry this morning. What are you doing here?"

"My life is in shambles."

"Again? What happened?"

"I danced ten hours a day, every day, for weeks. For what? Third place! Guess what third place gets you?"

"The bronzed dancing shoe trophy?"

"Nothing! Literally nothing. My agent hasn't received *anything*. It's seriously the most horrid thing to ever happen to me."

"What's with the elephant?"

"I bought it for Lilly at the airport. It's cute, right?"

Honestly, it was a little freaky looking. The eyes were the size of saucepans, and the body was the size of a small horse. Not sure where I'd store it, but I appreciated the gesture.

"Auntie Amy!" Lilly came barreling into the room and jumped onto the bed. "Ahhhh! What is that?" She pointed to the elephant.

"It's a present for you. Do you like it?"

"No. I hate it!"

"Why? Look. His name is"—Amy checked the tag—"Blimpo."

"He's scary." Lilly started to whimper and covered her eyes. "Make him go away!"

"How about we put Blimpo away for now." I removed the offending toy and shoved him into my closet. He barely fit.

"Talk about bursting my bubble," Amy said. "That thing was fifty bucks."

Lilly peeked between her fingers. Once she saw the giant elephant was gone, she perked back up and started jumping on the bed. "Hey, Auntie Amy. I saw you lose on TV."

"Thanks for the reminder, kid." Amy stood, grabbed Lilly, and swung her up on her hip. Amy and I had been best friends since the third grade. We grew up in Fresno and moved to Los Angeles when she decided to be an actress. I'd tagged along because that's what I do. I'm a tagger-alonger. Amy was tall and thin and had blonde hair. Like ninety-two percent of all C-list actresses in Los Angeles. Which is why she added in colorful highlights to differentiate herself. Today, she had teal tips and pink streaks.

"How long have you been here?" I asked.

"A few hours. I had to know why you've been ghosting me."

"I haven't been *ghosting* you." Unless ghosting meant not returning text or calls—then, yeah, I was ghosting her.

"All I know is that I saw you at the party after the finale. Then I get a text from you three days later with the shocked face emoji, barf face emoji, two flowers, and an upside-down smiley face. What does that mean?"

"I don't remember." Which was the truth. "Shouldn't you be home with your boyfriend?"

"He's at a dental conference in San Diego. Don't change the subject. What happened in New York?"

"I'm hungry," Lilly announced.

"And I will feed you, child," I said, grateful for the interruption.

"Not so fast, Clyne." Amy followed me down the hallway, Lilly still on her hip. "I want to know what happened."

I opened the fridge and pulled out the bread and butter. "We had a nice trip."

"Can me have sparkle toast?" Lilly slipped out of Amy's arms and went to the fridge. By sparkle, she meant raspberry jam.

"What happened?" Amy demanded.

I dropped the bread into the toaster and set the dial.

Amy drummed her fingers on the freshly polished counter. "I am literally not leaving until you tell me. I know that face. Something bad happened." She gasped. "Oh hell, are you pregnant?"

"You're pregnant!" Lilly cheered. "Yay! I get a baby sister!"

I shot Amy a look. "No, I am *not* pregnant, and let's not say that out loud, please."

"Are you sure?" Amy asked. "Because the last time you made that face was when you were pregnant with Lilly. Did Chase knock you up?"

"What does knock up mean?" Lilly asked.

Oh, geez. "It's um…when you…um…" I was not prepared for this conversation.

"It's when you get a knock on the noggin." Amy made a fist and lightly tapped herself on the head.

Lilly made a face. "That doesn't sound good. I don't ever want Mommy to be knocked up."

Oh, geez.

The toaster dinged. I pulled out the toast and added butter and "sparkle."

"Cambria!" Amy was growing impatient. I couldn't blame her. We talked about everything, but I wasn't ready to divulge the details of my disastrous trip. Mostly because I wasn't ready to deal with the aftermath. Not yet.

"I promise I'll tell you everything once I've had time to process." There were things I had to figure out on my own without Amy's input. She had a lot of opinions when it came to my love life.

"Wow. Was it that bad?"

"Yep." I cut Lilly's toast in half and walked it over to the table.

"What's with the back of your legs," Amy asked. "Are those hickeys and a rash?"

"They're goat bites, and I fell into insulation. It's been a rough day."

"Your job is weird."

"We had a mishap at the Burbank property today." I stepped into the office, to get out of Lilly's earshot, and Amy followed. "A dead person was found in the attic."

Amy's eyes went wide. "You found a dead person. Again?"

"I didn't find it," I said, keeping my voice low. "A resident found the body shoved into a barrel. Police said she could have been there for *years*."

"That's disgusting." She did a full body shiver. "No more details, please."

"The thing is, they'll use dental records to identify her, but if they can't, they'll release the story to the public to see if anyone else can help identify the victim."

"Why is that a problem?"

"I ended up interviewing next door, and they will not want to hire me if I'm involved in a high-profile murder investigation. Not after what happened to their last manager."

"I can see their point. If they want to stay away from scandal, they shouldn't hire you. You're cursed."

"So I've heard."

"Why don't you look at the missing person website to see if there's anyone who matches the description of the victim?" Amy asked.

"That's a brilliant idea."

"You're welcome." She rolled a chair up to my desk, and we started the search. Turns out there are an alarming number of missing people in California.

"The person was female and petite with brown hair." I scrolled through the pictures.

"Well, that narrows it down," Amy said with a roll of her eyes.

Amy's sarcasm was in reference to the fact half of the people on the missing person list were petite females with brown hair. But none of the dates lined up. There were two women from the sixties, one from the late seventies, and the rest were from within the last five years.

I grabbed a scrap of paper and wrote down the names anyway. Francis Holland, Tammy Whitewood, and Larissa Lopez. I didn't bother with the women who went missing recently. Even an untrained eye could tell that body had been there a long time.

I should probably call Patrick to discuss what happened. So I did.

"You found another dead body?" he asked after I told him the story. Apparently, Hampton had not talked to him yet. Oops.

"No, I didn't find any body. Fox did."

"It's distressing how many dead people have turned up since you were hired."

I hoped that wasn't his opening line when the Dashwoods called to verify employment.

"For the record," I said, "this body was clearly there prior to my taking over. Perhaps it's not that people have died since I showed up—it's that I'm more observant than the managers before me."

He made a sound. I couldn't tell if it was sigh or a grunt, or if he was crying. Could have been all three. Patrick had said at least a hundred times since I'd started that he'd spent too many years in property management. He was burned out. I could tell. Lucky for me, he was too young to retire. Thank goodness. If he did quit, we'd all be out of a job.

"Have you ever been in the attic?" I asked.

"No, there's never been a reason to."

"Have you ever been in the attic here?"

"No, there's never been a reason to."

Note to self: Check the attic here for dead bodies.

Scratch that. My eyes had already seen too much.

Note to self: Look into hiring a company who comes out to look for corpses.

"According to the police, the body looked to have been dead anywhere from twenty to thirty years, and it was a petite female with brown hair."

There was silence on the other end. So much so, I thought Patrick had hung on me. "Hello?"

"I'm here," he finally said.

"Chase is going to contact the McMillses. Do you know if they've talked?"

"I'm sure if the McMillses knew about a dead person in the attic, I would have heard. I think they took their yacht to Mexico. I don't know if they're back yet. I'll call Trevor in the morning."

I thought a dead body warranted a call tonight. But I wasn't about to tell Patrick how to do his job.

"Do you think Mr. or Mrs. McMills hid the body there?"

"The McMillses have a lot of money. They could find a better place to dispose of a body than in the attic of their own property."

You'd think so, but I added the McMillses to the list of suspects I'd already mentally prepared anyway. Patrick had taken over management twenty-five years ago, and as far as I knew, the McMillses didn't have a prior management company. They had done everything themselves.

I ran this information by Patrick to double check.

"They had onsite apartment managers," he said. "But they didn't have a management company until I was hired. After Trevor graduated law school, he took over the trust, and I haven't spoken to the McMillses since. I don't know how involved they were in the day-to-day running of the properties before I got there. I do know the Burbank apartments had problems with wild tenants. There was a lot of turnover, not much enforcement of the house rules, and I heard there was a big drug problem. Mostly pot."

"I brought home files from the past few residents of the apartments with attic access," I said. "There aren't that many. Can I get the archives for the Burbank building?"

I could almost hear Patrick shaking his head. "Trevor McMills has all the files."

"Can you ask if I can have a look?"

"I'll ask. Why don't you let the police handle this?"

"Because...um...like I said, I'm much more observant. Plus, with cops there, I can't very well rent out Apartment 14B, and I hate vacancies." This was all true. Not my main motive, but absolutely true.

"You're committed—I'll give you that much."

"You know you couldn't do this without me." I regretted the statement as soon as it left my mouth. Why would I tell him this right before I quit?

Smart, Cambria. Real smart.

"You're right," Patrick said, and I felt like crap. "Curious, did the police say if they had any leads?"

"They didn't say. Can you think of any petite females who went missing?"

"I think I can be counted on to remember if a resident vanished," he said.

"I doubt it was a resident. I'm thinking it was a friend or acquaintance of someone who lived there. Any tenants who gave off a murderous vibes?"

"I remember hearing stories about unruly roommates in Apartment 2B. Two younger guys who worked in the film industry. They were known for their parties, and drugs. And they'd bring home a lot of women."

"What happened to them?"

"The McMillses gave them notices to vacate right before I got there. As a matter of fact, their old apartment was the first one we leased under Elder Property Management."

Two young guys having parties, bringing women home, and doing drugs seemed like a good lead. Their information would be in the archives. I *really* needed to get ahold of those.

"Speaking of unruly tenants," Patrick said, "have you spoken to Kevin?"

"No!" Oops. I cleared my throat. "I mean, *no.*" Kevin was the McMills's estranged son, and the occupant of Apartment 40 at the Los Angeles building.

"Didn't he go to New York with you?"

"*Yes*?"

"Was that a question or an answer?"

"Answer?"

"If you see him, have him call me back, please."

"I'll do that?"

Amy gave me a sideways glance. I turned in my chair to face the window.

"Please let me know about the archives," I said. "Thanks, Patrick. Bye." I hung up and opened my desk drawer. Not because I needed anything, but because I didn't want Amy to see my face.

"Did something happen with Kevin?" she asked.

I rearranged my bottom drawer, starting with the stacks of envelopes.

"Cambria?"

"Man, I really need to throw some of this stuff away."

"Cambria!"

I could feel Amy breathing down my neck.

"Mommy!" Lilly called out. "Mommy, I'm done!" She skipped into the office. She looked like the Joker, with raspberry jam extending from the corners of her mouth. "Do you like my new doll, Auntie Amy? It's the Statute of Liberty."

"Statue," I corrected while wiping her face using a tissue.

"Don't you think it's pretty, Auntie Amy?" Lilly shoved the plush toy up to Amy's face.

"It's so cool," Amy said with forced enthusiasm. "Creepier than my elephant, but whatever. Did your mommy bring this back for you?"

"No. My daddy gave it to me."

I could feel Amy's eyes beating into the side of my skull, so I continued to look busy by checking my phone to see if Chase had texted me back. Still no reply.

"Did your daddy go to New York, too?" Amy asked Lilly.

Three-year-olds *cannot* keep secrets.

"I dunno if he did or not."

Which is why we don't tell her *anything*.

"Cambria Jane Clyne." Amy turned my chair, forcing me to face her. "Did Tom go to New York?"

"*No.*"

"You're lying! There's no way he just so happened to buy her a Statue of Liberty doll. When did he go to New York?"

I decided it was time to dust the counter.

"Ooohhh, I see how it is." Amy tapped her foot. "Looks like the girl in the barrel isn't the only mystery that needs to be solved around here."

I knew no matter how hard she tried, Amy would never figure out what had transpired. I was still trying to figure it out myself, and until I did: *mum's the word.*

.

CHAPTER FOUR

Can prepare pertinent market surveys

My grandma Ruthie used to say, "There is no better medication than a good night's rest." Which is great, except my brain doesn't have a power off button. I woke up in a bad mood. Ignoring my sore calf, I stomped to the office to start my day. There were several housekeeping items to deal with (rent, deposits, filing paperwork, going through messages, normal everyday manager stuff), before I could dive deeper into the woman in the barrel. Amy was snoozing on my couch, having stuck to her promise of not leaving until she knew what happened in New York. During our friendship, we'd mostly dealt with her relationship problems, not mine. She'd talk about it in an obsessive manner until the issue had passed.

Me?

Avoidance was my coping mechanism of choice when it came to dealing with issues of the opposite sex.

And by avoidance I meant investing in a good spy movie, or binging my favorite crime show *If Only,* or eating ice cream. *Not* solving a murder. But that was what I had to work with.

Oh, and the ice cream.

Mint chip felt like a suitable breakfast. Dairy for my bones. Mint for my digestive system. Chocolate for my mood. I'd call that well-balanced.

After looking more carefully over the files I'd brought home, I realized the barrel was located right above Apartment 4B. I waited until 8 a.m. to call the current resident, who had lived there for over twenty years. The conversation was riveting.

Me: Have you ever gone into the attic?
Resident: There's an attic?

Me: Yes, there's attic access in your hallway.
Resident: Where in the hallway?
Me: In the ceiling.
Resident: Huh?

So that was a bust. My best bet was the resident prior, May Ashburd, who moved into the apartment in 1990 and moved out in 1996.

"And who are you again?" May asked for the third time since she'd answered.

"My name is Cambria Clyne, and I manage the apartment building in Burbank, where you used to live."

"That place was a dive." May had the voice of a woman who'd punch you in the face if you looked at her wrong.

"I'm happy to report it's turned around over the last few years. I'm calling because I'm curious if you ever happened to look in the attic?"

"Why?"

Excellent question. "I'm conducting a survey."

The line went silent.

"Hello?"

I heard a door close, followed by the distinct slam of a toilet seat. "I may have peeked up there a few times," May finally said.

"What did you see?"

"There were big metal barrels. Made me nervous. What if there was an earthquake? They could fall through the ceiling and land on my head!"

I felt like May and I could be friends, because that would have been my first thought. "How many were there?"

"Five of them, right above my apartment."

The toilet flushed, and I pretended not to notice because May held useful information. "Why did you look up there?"

May washed her hands. I could hear the faucet running in the background. "I had neighbors from hell. They were loud, threw parties, had obnoxious friends, and they would drag big bags up and down the stairs at all hours of the night. They'd store those bags in the attic. They even had someone sleeping up there once."

I thought back to the pillow I'd found near the barrel. "What apartment number was this?"

"Apartment 2B. Alvin and Sherman. I never forget the names of people who annoyed the hell out of me."

I shuffled through the stack of folders I'd brought home. No Alvin or Sherman. These must be the roommates Patrick mentioned. "Did you tell the manager?"

"We had a few managers come and go, and none of them did anything. I'd see Mr. McMills there all the time, and I told him what Alvin and Sherman were up to. He gave a notice to all tenants saying we weren't allowed to go into the attic. Finally, he kicked them out right before the new management company took over."

This was a great lead. "After Alvin and Sherman moved out, did you happen to look in the attic?"

"Sure did." May's voice sounded far away, and I could hear dishes clanking in the background. She was quite productive when on the phone. "A few months before I moved out, I heard a scraping noise across the ceiling in the middle of the day. I worked nights back then at Warner Brothers, cleaning studios, and it woke me up. I checked to see what the Sam Hill was going on. And all those barrels were gone."

"All but one, right?"

"I didn't see *any*." So the barrels were moved after Patrick took over management. However, he claimed to have never been in the attic. How was he able to have the barrels moved if he didn't know they existed?

"Do you know where the barrels were taken to?" I asked.

"Not a dang clue."

Shoot.

"But I do know that the maintenance guy had to go up there *a lot*," May said. "He'd give me a day's notice, saying he had to use the attic access in my apartment. So damn annoying."

Interesting, but not suspicious. Anyone proficient with tools and construction wouldn't have built a wall with plywood and tape. Of course, if a person were desperate and rushed and had just killed a woman, they might not be in the right frame of mind to construct a wall...

Note to self: Check maintenance logs.

"Do you remember what month the barrels were moved?" If I could get my hands on the work orders, then I could see who moved them, where they went, and if one was left behind.

"It would have been September. What kind of survey is this, anyway?"

"A market survey," I said, which made absolutely no sense. Market surveys were conducted to collect information on rental prices and vacancies from other managers. Lucky for me, May didn't ask any questions. Instead, she continued to wash her dishes until I thanked her for her time and we hung up.

Alvin and Sherman jumped to the top of my suspect list. A small part of me wanted to add Patrick's name right under the McMills's. I couldn't imagine Patrick killing anyone, but I'd been deceived before by people I trusted. If I were to find large barrels in the attic at either of the properties I managed, I would call Patrick before I moved them. Heck, if I owned a management company, and I was taking over a building, I'd do a full tour of all attics and storage closets to make sure everything was in order.

Of course, May's timing could have been off, and maybe the barrels were gone before Patrick took over.

I decided to call Patrick and run this by him. His voice mail answered on the first ring, and his mailbox was full. It wasn't like Patrick to not check his voice mails.

I sent a text message instead, asking Patrick to call me back, and reminding him to ask Trevor McMills about the archived files. I'd like to take a look before Hampton and Chase used their badges to confiscate everything.

I turned off my computer, put a sign in the window saying I'd return at one, and went into the apartment. Lilly was perched on Amy's back—who was still asleep—watching cartoons with the Statue of Liberty doll on her lap.

"Why is her asleep on my couch?" Lilly asked.

"It's *she*, and Aunt Amy is having a hard time dealing with the real world."

"Shhhh!" Amy scolded and put the pillow over her head. "It's too early."

"You ready to go rent apartments?" I tried to sound excited.

I should have tried harder.

Lilly responded with an exaggerated sigh. Accompanying me to work was not her favorite thing to do, and I couldn't blame her. No three-year-old wanted to be dragged around on apartment tours. Lucky for her (and me), this was her last day on the job. She started preschool tomorrow. We'd found a safe and somewhat affordable place right around the corner. I didn't want to spend her last day of no school dealing with a dead body, but if I wanted to live next door, then I had to make sure this didn't get out. Which meant staying ahead of the gossip and finding out who was in the barrel.

Easier said than done.

Lilly and I got dressed. Me in jeans, a blue T-shirt, and white Converse (my usual attire), and Lilly in a Captain Marvel costume. As a parent, I'd learned to pick and choose my battles. There were worse things in the world than dressing like an Avenger.

We were gathering our stuff when there was a knock on the door.

Amy threw the blankets off her head. "Who is here so freaking early in the morning?"

I checked the peephole. "No one," I almost sang. "Go back to sleep."

"Where are you going?"

"To Burbank. Do you want to go shopping for a first day of school outfit for Lilly later?"

"Obviously."

"Good. I'll be back around one. Or you can go home, and I'll meet you at your place."

"What happened in New York?"

"Bye." I opened the door wide enough for Lilly and me to squeeze outside.

"Why are you sneaking out of your apartment?" Chase asked, standing in front of the door with a grocery bag and a pink donut box.

"Aunt Amy is having a hard time adjusting to the real world," said Lilly.

Chase looked to me for clarification.

"She's asleep on my couch. Boyfriend is out of town. Apparently, third place on *Celebrity Tango* doesn't do much for your career." I pushed past him, keeping my eyes on the carports.

Chase caught up. "What's the rush?"

"Amy doesn't know about New York, and I don't want to tell her," I said, low enough for Lilly not to hear.

We passed my upstairs neighbor Mickey, who was up and walking the property, muttering to himself—something about government conspiracies and corrupt cops—the usual. Chase, Lilly, and I stopped to wave then kept walking.

"Why aren't you telling Amy?" Chase asked.

"Because…wait a second." I suddenly remembered. "You never did text me back. Please, please, tell me you didn't agree to a double date with Hampton and Silvia."

"He's my partner."

"You didn't answer my question."

"I brought ice cream." He held up the bag. "Mint chip, french vanilla, rocky road, and double fudge."

I tried to roll my eyes, but I was only partially successful.

"And I came with news about the girl in the barrel," he said.

This got my attention. "What's the latest?"

Chase held up the bag and box. "Pick your poison. Ice cream or donut?"

"That bad?"

"You're going to want coping mechanisms."

Great.

My gut said, *"No, no, please no! Stop eating. Make it all go away."*

My mouth said, "Donut." I grabbed a glazed cruller, my favorite kind of donut and detective, *hehe.* "Go ahead and give it to me."

"Dental records won't be helpful in the case, because the victim didn't have teeth."

I went ahead and shoved the rest of the donut into my mouth and grabbed another. "Why the heck didn't she have teeth? Was she old?"

"No, preliminary results put her between thirty-five and forty."

The donut hit my stomach like a brick. Ugh. I felt awful. Poor thirty-something-year-old, petite, toothless woman. "Do you think the"—I looked down at Lilly, who had wrapped herself around my leg, and was intently paying attention—"the k-i-l-l-e-r removed the teeth?"

"Yes and no. She had bone resorption and two implant posts, which is consistent with someone who had a fixed denture. We think the killer removed her dentures."

"Thirty-something is young to have dentures. Right?" I ran my tongue across my teeth, trying to remember if I brushed this morning.

"There's more," Chase said. "They ruled the cause of death blunt force trauma to the head."

Oh man, this was getting worse by the minute. I knew from my crime shows that blunt force trauma to the head was typically a crime of passion. Which meant the victim was likely in a heated argument when she got clocked. A lovers' quarrel? An argument with a neighbor? The manager? The maintenance man? The owner of the building? Or had she been in one of the bags Sherman and Alvin dragged up to their apartment and stored in the attic?

"Do they have *any* idea who she was?" I asked.

"No. There was no identification on her. Fingerprints won't be helpful because the body is too badly decomposed. She was dressed too nice to be homeless. Her clothing dated her to the midnineties. They believe she was of Hispanic descent. No exact date on her death. It could take up to a year to gather more information. Hampton wanted me to give you a heads-up, because they're going to release the story to the press."

Great. Just great. What was I supposed to do, though? Justice was more important than a pay increase, financial security, nicer apartment, career advancement, and vision insurance.

"You're not even going to try to figure out who she was first?" That just sounded like lazy detective-ing to me.

"Of course we are, Cambria. We have very little to go off of right now. Hampton called Patrick and the McMillses, but he hasn't heard from either of them."

"The McMillses are on a yacht in Mexico, and I spoke to Patrick last night. He didn't know much. When is the story releasing?"

"Thursday."

"Thursday?" I perked up. "As in the day after tomorrow?"

"Yes, they want to run a few more tests. We're going to see how those pan out."

"I can work with Thursday! I already have a few leads."

Chase arched an eyebrow. "If you have leads, then you should give them to me."

"Probably a good idea. I'll text you the information I found out this morning about the roommates in Apartment 2B. The more people we have working on the case, the better."

"The LAPD is happy to assist you."

"Good." I winked and went in for a kiss, when Lilly smacked me on the stomach. "Ouch. What's wrong?"

"Can me go now?"

"It's *we*, and in a minute."

"Before you go"—Chase bent down and opened the pink box—"I picked out a unicorn donut just for you, Captain."

Lilly cowered behind me.

"What's wrong?" I asked.

"Nothing." She dug her face into my thigh. This was very unlike her. She loved Chase. Especially when he had sugar.

"Lilly." I tried to pry her off my leg, but she had a tight grip. "Come on, Lilly."

"Tell him to go away!"

"Lilly," I scolded. "Stop that."

"It's fine." Chase closed the box and stood up. "I get it," he said, but I could tell he was hurt. How could he not be?

"It's not fine." I pried Lilly off my leg and took a knee so I could be at eye level. She pouted her bottom lip, red in the cheeks. "It's not OK to be rude when grown-ups are talking to you. If you don't want a donut, that is fine. You say, 'no, thank you.'"

I could almost see the little wheels in her head turning. A part of me wanted to kiss her on the cheek because she was so dang cute, but I didn't want her to grow up to be a butthead. Los Angeles had enough of those walking around. I had to remain firm.

"Got it?" I tried again.

"OK." She looked up at Chase with her big hazel eyes. "Can you please go away forever? And can I have the unicorn donut, please?"

Horrified is the only word I could use to describe how I felt. I'd never seen Lilly be so rude towards anyone, let alone Chase, whom she adored.

At least, she used to adore.

"Here you go, Captain Marvel." He handed her the unicorn donut, which was really a glazed jelly-filled with rainbow sprinkles on top.

Lilly happily swiped her donut and danced over to my car, humming a celebratory tune.

"I'm so sorry," I said to Chase. "I have no idea why she'd say something like that."

"You don't?"

"No, I absolutely don't."

Chase nodded his head, as if answering an internal question. "Please text me all the information you have." He handed me the donut box and bag of ice cream. "I'll talk to you later." He walked back to his car, which was parked next to the maintenance garage.

I swiped a maple bar. Adulting is hard.

Lilly was already in her booster seat, buckled in, still humming, when I got in the car. I reattached the rearview mirror, pumped the gas a few times, turned the key, and we were on our way to the Burbank building. "Are you going to tell me why you said that to Chase?" I asked, keeping my eyes on the road. Morning traffic was a beast.

"'Cause I want him to go away forever," she said matter-of-factly.

"Do you not like Chase?"

"I like hims."

"It's *him*. Did he hurt your feelings?"

"No. Hims is very nice."

"*He*. Then why did you tell him to go away forever? That really hurt his feelings."

"'Cause I was thinking it in my head, and then it came out of my mouth."

"Why was it in your head?"

I could hear her shrug her little shoulders as I inched onto the freeway behind a line of cars. I wanted to press for more details, but I knew the more I pressed, the more this would become "a thing." If I let it go, she could as well. There was no way Lilly had this thought on her own, though. Not at three years old. Someone must have said something, and I had a good idea who that someone was.

CHAPTER FIVE

———

Excellent time-management skills.

Fox was in the courtyard doing yoga when I arrived at the Burbank building. "I thought you were getting rid of the goats?" I asked.

"The guy doesn't take returns." Fox twisted his leg up and over his head. He had on fewer clothes today. Just a tank top and *short* neon-green shorts, leaving very little to the imagination.

"Wow, you are really flimsy," Lilly said. "And I like your pets."

"He's flexible," I corrected and pushed her aside, taking a protective stance should I need to fend off a goat attack. The brown goat was standing beside Fox while the white one was on his back. They appeared to be in a better mood—*ouch*!

Spoke too soon.

"Mother...bleepin!" I hobbled around, rubbing my leg. "The goats need to go, Fox."

"What if they're service animals?"

"Yoga isn't considered a service."

"Why not? I found a dead body, and I can't even tweet about it, so I'm doing my yoga. The goats help maximize my zen."

I opened my mouth then snapped it shut. Dammit! He had me there.

"Can I pet your goat?" Lilly reached out her hand, and I swung her up onto my hip.

"Don't touch her," I said.

"Why?"

"Because she bites."

"Why?"

"Because…just because."

Fox lowered into the splits. "The goats have been pretty chill. They just don't like you."

"Well, the feeling is mutual—*ouch!*" *Breathe. Breathe. Breathe through the pain.* "Fox," I said through gritted teeth.

"I'll find them a new home."

"Today," I grunted.

"As soon as I'm done. You ever heard of the Zankla books?"

"What?"

"They're about the Tarian people."

"What?"

"They're super hot right now."

"What?"

"I've got an audition tomorrow for the role of the goat shapeshifter in the Soldurian Clan."

Heaven help me, I had way too many starving actors in my life.

"I'm really feeling the character," he said. "It's a role I was born to play."

"Good luck." I limped up the stairs to Apartment 14B with Lilly still on my hip. The door didn't have a notice from the police, and I deemed it safe to enter.

"Ah! It's so hot!" Lilly fanned her face.

Agreed. It was like stepping directly into a convection oven. Holy hell! I opened all the windows, which would have helped if there were a breeze outside. But there wasn't.

I'd need to hurry. If it was hot in a second floor apartment, then it was going to be surface-of-the-sun hot in the attic. I wanted to check if there were more barrels up there.

The cable company's ladder was folded and up against the wall. Perfect.

Lilly stuck out her tongue like a dog. "Why is it so hot?"

"Because these units don't have air conditioners."

"Why?"

"Because the owners didn't have the place ducted."

"Why?"

"These are wonderful questions," I said. "Keep them in your head, and I'll answer them when we're done. OK?"

"Why?"

I handed her my phone.

"Yay!" She plopped down on the floor without another word. That should keep her busy for a few minutes. Still, I couldn't let her bake. So I ran downstairs, grabbed a fan from my office, hurried back, and plugged it in. Lilly was so engrossed in the show she was watching on Netflix, that she didn't even flinch when I picked her up and positioned her in front of the fan.

That's better.

I locked the door, set up the ladder, and climbed into the attic. As expected, it was stifling. Well over a hundred degrees. Sweat dripped from my forehead, and I did a quick look around, careful not to touch the pink stuff.

There were no other barrels up there. The pillow must have been collected and taken to the medical examiner. The previous resident, May, had said that Alvin and Sherman in Apartment 2B had a friend sleeping up here. She didn't say if the friend was male or female, and I wondered if the victim could have been crashing up there before she was killed.

There were a few sporadic windows, allowing for sunlight to peek in. I examined the corner where the barrel was. A dark ring had formed on the floor, and there were several deep gashes in the wood.

Apartment 4B, where May had lived, was directly below. The entry into the unit was roughly five feet away from where the barrel had been. I checked the framing around the access point, to see if it had been damaged. Nope. The wood looked perfectly intact. The opening was about an inch wider than the base of the barrel. It would be hard to remove them without causing damage.

There was a narrow walkway to the attic access point into Apartment 2B. Unlike 4B, the framing around the door was scuffed, chipped, and splintery. This was consistent with May's account of the two roommates frequently using the attic as their own personal storage facility.

I was sweaty, and a little light-headed. It was awfully hot up there, and I was mindful of the time, being that my phone was currently babysitting Lilly. I had to hurry. But first, there was a space with plywood flooring off to the side, and I ducked under a beam to check it out. A window allowed enough light in for me to see. Five rusty colored circles matching the one in the corner were stamped into the wood. The fact that the circles were so visible made me think those barrels had been there for a long time before they were removed.

This meant someone had to have moved four barrels, leaving the one with the woman behind. Why wouldn't they have taken the one with the victim? You'd think that would be a top priority. Surely, whoever stuffed her in there couldn't have thought it would be a permanent solution. The barrel sat atop wires, for goodness' sake. At some point in the future, those wires would have had to be replaced. It seemed to me that whoever moved the barrels had no idea there was a fifth hidden.

I climbed down, grabbed my phone from Lilly, settled her after she threw a massive fit, and we walked to my office. Fox and his goats were gone. I'd have to deal with that situation soon. Even if he considered them service animals, I'd need the documentation. His poor downstairs neighbors. I thought living beneath Mickey, who tromped across my ceiling several times a night to use the bathroom, was bad. I couldn't imagine two goats prancing around.

My cell rang. A number I didn't recognize flashed across the screen, and I answered. "Hello."

"It's Dr. Dashwood from Cedar Creek."

"Oh, hi." I closed the door and sat on the hard plastic folding chair at my desk. Lilly started to ask me a question, and I pressed my finger to her lips. She channeled her inner Captain Marvel and pretended to blast me with photons. "How can I help you, Dr. Dashwood?"

"We don't seem to have the right number for Patrick Elder. Can I get it from you?"

My stomach did a somersault. I really didn't want her talking to Patrick. But she couldn't hire me without speaking to my current employer. "Of course. Let me check." I tried not to sound as anxious as I felt. I should have told Patrick last night about the job interview so he wouldn't be blindsided when the Dashwoods called.

I went through my contacts and read off his work number.

"That's the one we have as well," Dr. Dashwood said. "But that line has been disconnected."

"Are you sure?" I rarely called Patrick on his work line, but I had used the number before, and it did work. Weird. "Let me give you his cell." I rattled off the numbers.

"Thank you. And while I have you on the phone, I've been doing research about what we talked about yesterday. Are you comfortable with heat, or should we do smaller sizes?"

Uh… "Huh?"

"You said you loved the idea," she said, her tone accusing.

"Oh yeah, right. Right. Yes. Of course. I think, um…smaller sizes are better?"

"I absolutely agree."

"Great." I wish I had a time machine. If I did, I'd travel to yesterday to see what I agreed to.

"Hopefully we can get ahold of Patrick today," she said. "We're anxious to get everything settled."

"Me, too."

"We'll be in touch. " She hung up, and I heaved a sigh.

First the full voice mail box and now the disconnected work line—certainly an odd coincidence.

I called Elder Property Management's office, and—sure enough—the number didn't work. I tried not to jump to conclusions (Patrick was the killer, and he fled the country, never to be heard from again), but it was really hard to keep my brain from going to the worst-case scenario.

I tried Patrick's cell phone, and the call went straight to a full mailbox. May's account of the barrels echoed through my mind. There were five, and right after Patrick took over management, they were taken away. Why were there barrels there in the first place? What was in them? More bodies?

"Can we go?" Lilly asked.

"Not yet, sweetie."

"This isn't fun."

She had me there. "A few more minutes." I yanked open the filing cabinet and searched for old maintenance logs. I found invoices dating back to the early nineties from a company called Handy Man Express. A handwritten work order was stapled to the back of each invoice. Most were for broken toilet seats, and all invoices were stamped PAST DUE in red. This was before Patrick took over. He always pays bills the moment they cross his desk.

A man named Neo Doukas signed off each work order. According to Google, Handy Man Express was no longer in business. A quick search on LinkedIn, and I was able to find Neo. He owned a restaurant in West Hollywood that—according to Yelp—had the most authentic Greek food in all of Hollywood. Convenient, because I could go for a gyro.

* * *

Greek House was located on Santa Monica Blvd. between a gelato shop and a Subway. I parked in the lot across the street. It was only ten o'clock, and the restaurant didn't open until eleven. I cupped my hands around my eyes and peered in through the window. Greek House was nothing more than a counter with a soda machine and a register with a grill along the back wall. The menu consisted of ten items, and there was only seating on the front patio. It didn't look like much, but I had a feeling the food was good. There was no way Neo could afford the rent on Santa Monica Blvd. if it weren't.

I could see that the back door was open, and I walked around to the alleyway, holding Lilly's hand.

"Are we here to buy me new clothes?" she asked.

"Not yet. We'll go shopping later. First, I need to speak to someone. It shouldn't take long."

She thunked the heel of her hand against her forehead. It was cute. So I stopped to take a picture.

There was a young guy—late teens/midtwenties (I sucked at age guesstimation)—unloading boxes from a delivery truck.

"I'm looking for Neo Doukas," I said to the boy. He had dark, curly hair and thick eyebrows. His shirt had Greek House printed on the front, and his name tag said Neo. But he didn't match the profile picture on LinkedIn, and he was about thirty years too young to be the Neo I was looking for.

"My dad's in the office," he said.

I thanked him and stepped around the tower of boxes. The office was at the end of the hall next to the bathroom. The door was wide open, and sitting behind the desk was a handsome older man with wisps of gray hair, dark eyes, and a round nose. He was looking over paperwork, and I tapped on the door with my knuckles to grab his attention.

"My name is Cambria Clyne," I said once he looked up. "I manage an apartment building in Burbank where Handy Man Express used to work. I found several invoices with your name on them, and I wanted to ask you a few questions."

I could tell by the expression on Neo's face that he had no idea what to make of me. "I don't do handy work anymore."

"That's fine. What I need from you is information."

"I worked at a lot of apartment buildings in Burbank. You're gonna need to refresh my memory."

Right. If only our apartment building had a name. "It's managed by Elder Property Management now, but before they took over, the McMillses ran the place."

"*Oh,* I remember the McMillses," he said with a snort. "Ernest and Dolores McMills were the cheapest rich people I've ever met, and they never paid on time." Neo gestured to the chair on the opposite side of his desk, and I sat down, sliding Lilly onto my lap.

"And I see you brought Wonder Woman with you," Neo said, looking at Lilly. He reminded me of my grandpa. Rough voice, kind eyes, bushy brows.

Lilly stuck her fingers into her mouth, as she often did when deciding to be shy.

"She's Captain Marvel," I said. "Sorry to show up like this, but do you remember moving barrels from the attic when you worked for the McMillses?"

Neo steepled his fingers under his chin. "I remember there being barrels up there, but I didn't move them."

Shoot. "Did you ever look inside?"

"All the time. There were five of them leftover from the contractors who built the complex. Ernest didn't throw *anything* away. Most were empty; some were filled with various materials."

"Various things like a human?"

Neo's eyes opened wide. "No, various things like steel, extra tiles, wood, nails, and rocks. I would remember if there was a person inside. Are you a cop?"

"No, I'm an apartment manager with a c-o-r-p-s-e in the attic." I didn't want to have to explain to Lilly what a corpse was. My life would get a whole lot trickier once she learned to spell. "The c-o-r-p-s-e was a woman shoved into a barrel and hidden behind a makeshift wall. Looked like she'd been there for a long time."

"*How* long?"

"They don't know for sure, but at least twenty-five to thirty years. She was in her thirties, with dark hair, Hispanic, and she had dentures. Sound familiar?"

Neo just stared at me. "I don't remember anyone fitting that description. We had a lot of turnover there. The tenants were loud and liked to party. I fished bras out of the palm tree more times than I care to remember."

It was hard to imagine the Burbank property as a frat house. Then again, when I first took over the Los Angeles property, it was unknowingly a crack house. "Do you remember Alvin and Sherman in Apartment 2B?"

"How can I forget? They were young set designers. Cocky little crapheads. They'd lug black bags up to their apartment and break the stairs. I had to replace several steps."

"I heard they stored those bags in the attic. Do you know what was inside?"

He shook his head. "I know they had someone sleeping up there for a while."

"What year was this?"

"That was in the nineties. Ernest finally kicked them out after that. I bet if the friend had been willing to pay rent, Ernest would have let him stay up there, though."

"And you're sure all those barrels were there the entire time you worked at the property?"

"Positive. And there weren't any barrels hidden in the walls either. We would have found it when re-wiring the place for internet."

"When did you stop working there?" I asked, afraid he'd say when Elder Property Management took over.

"When Elder Property Management took over. Happens a lot when new management companies come on. They have their own people."

Crap.

"I was done with the property management business anyway. *This* was my dream." He gestured to his office. "Best Greek food in Los Angeles."

Based on the aroma permeating from the kitchen, I believed him. My stomach growled. Before I could go stuff my face, I had to get to the bottom of the barrel.

"What was Ernest McMills like?" All I knew about the McMillses was that they disowned their only son after he announced he was gay. Other than that, I knew they were rich, and they apparently had a yacht. That was the depth of my knowledge when it came to the McMillses.

"He was a nice enough guy. Hated parting with money. I was shocked when they said that they'd hired a management company and were grooming their nephew to take over everything."

"Why?"

"Because he'd have to share his profits. I know they were having trouble with their son at the time, but I was still surprised."

I did the math in my head and realized the McMillses hired Elder Property Management right around when they kicked Kevin out and sent him to live at the Los Angeles property, rent free, so long as he never contacted them. There might be more to that story.

"And you're sure the barrels were still there when you left?"

Please say no. Please say no. Please say no.

"Positive."

Dang it.

This didn't necessarily mean Patrick had something to do with the murder. There was still Alvin and Sherman, who left right before Patrick was hired, and the McMillses, who owned the buildings. If Ernest was as cheap as Neo made him out to be, then he wouldn't have been OK with Patrick tossing the barrels.

"Are we almost *done*?" Lilly pulled on my shirt. "I want to go."

"We will soon." I kissed her on the top of the head and handed her my phone, because I was a good mother like that.

"You should talk to Reena Hike. She was the onsite property manager for the McMillses right before Elder took over."

"Reena Hike," I repeated, and grabbed my phone from a pouting Lilly. "According to Google, there are several Reena Hikes. One is an author."

"That's her."

"Really?" I turned my phone around to show him the picture of Reena, a *New York Times* best-selling paranormal romance author. She had dark skin, purple streaked hair, and long lashes. "She writes the Zankla Books." I was reading her bio. "A fictional series about the lives of the shape-shifting Tarian people who live in an apartment building in Borbank." I looked up at Neo. "Borbank?"

"Yes. *Bor*bank. The main character's name is Zankla, and she's the apartment manager."

Subtle.

I looked down at my phone. According to the internet, the twelfth book in the Zankla series released today, and there was a book signing event in Hollywood.

I can extend my lunch break a little longer.

It wasn't like my boss would know, since he was currently MIA.

CHAPTER SIX

———

Prioritizes tasks accordingly

I picked Amy up, and we drove to the book signing for Reena Hike on Hollywood Boulevard. Typically, I avoided Hollywood & Highland at all costs, especially during the summer months. There were tourists five people deep on both sides of the streets, stopping to take a picture of a star on the sidewalk. Stopping to take a picture with their favorite homeless person dressed as a superhero. Stopping to take a picture in front of the Dolby Theater. Stopping to take a picture in front of the Jimmy Kimmel studio…

Basically, there was a lot of stopping happening, and as a Los Angeleno, I was programed not to stop for anything or anyone at any time. Head down. Zero eye contact. Feet moving. There was someplace to be. And that someplace was a store called Horror Eclipse. We were fifteen minutes early, and there was already a line of people waiting outside. Most of them had blue faces and purple hair with blood dripping from their necks. I hoped this had something to do with the books.

Amy, Lilly, and I got in line. "I have never heard of Reena Hike." Amy used her hand as a fan. "And why is Lilly dressed like Captain Marvel?"

"Because why not?"

Amy inspected her nail beds. "It's popleie out today. I need a Xanax."

"You're the one who said you wanted to come."

She shrugged. "I wasn't doing anything else."

"Also, when did you start taking Xanax?"

"When I came in third place on *Celebrity Tango*." She gazed over her shoulder. "All these tourists, and not one person has recognized me. Look at them." She pointed to a group of people huddled on the corner, taking pictures of the Hollywood & Vine sign. "Hi!" She waved to get their attention. "Former television star and contestant on *Celebrity Tango* right here."

They stared at her for a moment then continued to take pictures of the sign.

Amy gestured to the tourists, her mouth open. "See what I mean?"

"First off, they're speaking in German. I don't think they understood you. Second, everyone knows that celebrities don't hang out on Hollywood Boulevard, so they might not believe you. Third, you're wearing a baseball cap and ginormous sunglasses. *I* barely recognize you."

"Oh." She went to remove the hat and paused. "I can't have too much sun exposure. You know, wrinkles."

"I like your purple hair," Lilly said to the man standing in front of us.

"Thanks, kid," he said. "Which species are you rooting for?"

"Cats."

"I am for the goat shifters."

"Ohhhh, yeah, I like cats. But they make my mom pee her pants."

I laughed a *kids-say-the-darnedest-things* type of laugh.

"When did you pee your pants?" Amy asked.

"I don't know what she's talking about." Fine, it had happened *one* time, and it was only because I'd read online that you should drink a gallon of water a day, and this was before I realized my bladder was not designed to hold so much liquid. A resident came in with a cat. I sneezed, and the rest is self-explanatory.

"What are these books about, anyway?" Amy asked.

"From the blurb, they sound like a passive-aggressive ode to her former job."

There was a tap on my shoulder, and I turned around. The woman behind us had blue paint smeared on her face and a green circle in the middle of her forehead. "I couldn't help but overhear you two talking. You haven't read the Zankla books?"

"No, we're new to the genre," I said.

The woman trembled with excitement, clutching a book in her hands. "I wish I could experience the Tarian people for the first time again. I'm a book blogger and received an advanced copy from the publisher of the latest installment. It's fantastic."

"Can I see that?" Amy asked, and the woman handed over the book. "So this is basically about a manager who is running an apartment building filled with wackos in Borbank," she said, reading the back. "Sound familiar?"

"Vaguely."

"Looks pretty good, actually. I wonder if they're going to make it into a movie."

We shuffled forward as the line began to move. "They are," I said. "One of my residents is auditioning tomorrow."

"You don't say." Amy opened to Chapter One. "*I stood outside the apartment building. How hard could this really be, I thought. Little did I know that I'd just signed my life away…* Dang, girl, this could be your autobiography!"

"Ain't that the truth."

We moved up in line, and more blue-faced people gathered behind us.

"I'm going to get myself a copy." Amy took out her phone. "Buying the ebook right now…aaannnddd…bought. Except, crap." She frowned. "How is she going to sign my iPhone?"

Lilly tugged on the bottom of my shirt. "When are we going to get clothes for my school?"

"Today," I promised. "Once we're done."

Lilly folded her arms. "Is this about the lady who was hit in the head and put in a barrel?"

Uhhhh.

I looked at Amy, and we both shrugged. "Sure," we said in unison.

Amy leaned in. "What are you hoping to accomplish with this apartment manager?"

"More information on the roommates who lived there, the McMillses, and the barrels in the attic."

"What does Kevin have to say about all this?"

"Where is Kevin?" Lilly asked. "Me haven't seen him."

"Me either," Amy said. "Why hasn't he been over?"

I took the opportunity to inspect the sky.

"The last time I saw Kevin was the night of the finale," Amy said. "When exactly did Tom arrive?"

"I want Chase to go away forever," Lilly blurted out.

Right. Need to deal with that.

Amy looked at me. "Well, that's new."

"Yeah," I whispered. "I'm trying not to give it life."

"He needs to find another place to go," Lilly said, wagging her finger.

Amy put her mouth up to my ear. "Pretty sure it already has life."

Pretty sure she was right.

Amy bent down to be face-to-face with Lilly. "I thought you loved Chase. Why do you want him to go away?"

"'Cause I was just thinking it."

"Sure, but who put the thoughts in your head?"

"No one! I just want him to go away and not be near my mommy."

I pinched the bridge of my nose.

Amy stood. "T-O-M."

"My thoughts exactly." If Tom was using our child to carry out his plan, then he had crossed a line—again.

Speaking of a line… We finally made it inside. The Horror Eclipse had brick walls, and pictures of Michael Meyers hung around the store. A six-foot stuffed clown towered near the cash register.

"I like this place. Can you buy me clothes here?" Lilly asked.

I was not about to send my daughter to preschool wearing a shirt with Freddy Krueger on the front.

"Please, Momma."

"Not here."

"But I like that one." She pointed to a shirt with Elvira's face on it. "She's so fancy."

"We'll go to Target and buy you something really pretty."

"Oh, come on," Amy said. "You let your kid prance around Hollywood dressed as Captain Marvel, and you won't let her wear a shirt with the Mistress of the Dark on it?"

"I don't see the correlation."

"She can't shop at *Target*," Amy said, as if the very thought was absurd, when I was ninety-nine percent positive her hat came from an end cap clearance rack at *Tarjay*. "She'll look like every other kid at school. Here." Amy dug through a pile of kids' apparel. "I'll get you this one." She held up a black shirt with the Munsters on the front.

"Yay! Auntie Amy is my favorite."

I started to protest, mostly because I imagined Lilly in a cute dress with a big bow in her hair on her first day of school.

But, whatever.

Amy and Lilly scooted off to the register to buy the shirt while I waited. I checked my phone. Two new text messages. One from Silvia, wanting to confirm our dinner plans for Friday. The second from Patrick. Hallelujah!

Patrick: I've taken the day off. Trevor said no to the archived files.

I was relieved to know he hadn't snuck off to Mexico to avoid persecution. But bummed Trevor said no to the files. What was the point of keeping archives if I wasn't allowed to look through them when needed?

"Excuse me. Excuse me." A man wearing black lipstick stood on a chair to get everyone's attention. "I'm sorry, folks," he said, and the room fell silent. "Ms. Hike had to leave early due to an urgent personal matter. We've made arrangements for her to return tomorrow at seven p.m. I have tickets here for you. Please present yours tomorrow night, and you'll be escorted to the front of the line."

What urgent matter could Reena Hike possibly have that would take her away from her own release day book signing?

CHAPTER SEVEN

———

Conflict Resolution

On the way home, my phone rang. It was Chase. My car had zero Bluetooth capability, and I was forced to pull over into a 7-11 parking lot. After what had happened with Lilly, I was anxious to talk to him.

"I'm so glad you called." I plugged one ear to hear him better over the traffic. "I'm sorry about this morning."

"There's no need to apologize, Cambria. I understand." Glad he did, because I didn't.

"But that's not why I called."

Oh.

"We haven't been able to get ahold of Patrick. Have you talked to him?"

Shoot.

"I haven't *talk* talked to him." I leaned against the hood of my car. Amy and Lilly were inside getting a Slurpee. "He replied to a text message."

"He hasn't replied to mine," Chase said. "What are you doing?"

"A little of this and a little of that. Do you know a Reena Hike?"

"The author who writes the Zankla series?"

"You've heard of them, too?"

"Hampton is a big fan. He listens to them on audiobooks. Why?"

"She used to manage the Burbank building. Sounds like her books are based on her time there. We tried to meet her, but she ran off on an *urgent* personal errand. You should talk to her."

"I'll look into it. Right now, I'm trying to find Patrick and the McMillses. Their yacht is docked, but we can't find them."

"I don't know about the McMillses, but Patrick has taken the day off."

"Convenient."

"Not really, because I have a lot of questions for him."

"I was being facetious."

"So was I." Not really. His joke went over my head, only because I was preoccupied. I really did not want Patrick to be involved in the murder.

Honestly. Could this situation get any worse?

"Silvia made us dinner reservations for Friday," Chase said. "And they want to see a movie afterwards."

I guess it could.

"I've decided to be sick on Friday," I said. "And contagious. Probably terminal."

"He's my partner, Cambria."

"And your partner's girlfriend started a rumor that I had a threesome with geriatric residents. One cancels out the other. I think it's against company policy to double date with a resident."

Note to self: Look into that.

"Please, Cambria." His voice was so soft and sincere— how could I say no?

So I went ahead and changed the subject. "I don't want Patrick to be a suspect."

"I don't either. But when he decides to go missing a day after a body is discovered on one of his properties, then he becomes a person of interest."

I was afraid he'd say that.

"What about the information on the roommates I texted you this morning?" I said. "Alvin and Sherman?"

"Do you have last names?"

"No. But how many Alvin and Shermans could there be in Burbank?"

"Over two thousand."

Oh.

"I'll see what I can do with first name and old address. We'll get to it, Cambria. I know how badly you want this solved. I do, too. Don't worry."

How could I not worry? Chase wasn't going to look at anyone else while Patrick was decidedly missing. I had no choice but to get ahold of those archives. Which meant I had to face someone I was not ready to.

The thought made me instantly nauseated.

CHAPTER EIGHT

Can easily handle difficult tasks.
...Mostly

I stood in front of Apartment 40, my stomach in knots. The television was on. I could see the flashing lights against the curtains covering the front window. Kevin had recently lost his job after a spontaneous trip to New York with me on what was supposed to be a fun get-away-from-our-problems excursion. The plan was for him to spend a few days as the third wheel with Chase and me, watch the *Celebrity Tango* finale. Then after Chase left, Kevin and I were supposed to sightsee for the remainder of the week.

If only the trip had gone as planned.

I knocked on the door. The television muted, and I could hear Kevin walk across his living room. I suspected he was wearing socks and underwear only. Kevin had this thing about clothing—he didn't like it.

My suspicion was confirmed when he opened the door wearing nothing but socks and underwear.

"Well, well, well, look who it is." He crossed his arms over his furry chest and smirked. Kevin McMills had auburn hair peppered with a few strands of gray, his face had strong masculine features, there was a tattoo of a snake on his arm, and he wore diamond studs in his ears. When I first started as the onsite property manager there, I considered Kevin my fortysomething man-child.

Now, we were friends.

At least we had been.

"Where's the kid?" he asked.

"With Amy back at my apartment, having dinner."

"What do you want?"

I shifted my eyes to the ground. "I need your help."

"You need *my* help? Haven't I helped you enough?"

"Yeah, yeah, just get it over with."

He placed a hand over his heart, feigning ignorance. "Get what over with?"

I heaved a sigh and waited.

"Oh, I suppose you're referring to the fact that you ditched me in Vegas!"

"To be fair, I left a note."

"I can't buy a plane ticket with a washed-out napkin with *sorry for last night. see you back home* written on it. Can I?"

"I wasn't going to pay for your plane ticket anyway. And it was your idea to leave New York early and extend our layover in Vegas."

"Yes, but it was your idea to visit the strip club, and that's when everything went to hell."

Strip club? "We didn't go to a strip club."

"Yes, we did. Right after we left the bar at Circus Circus."

Oh, right.

The night came back to me in waves of humiliation…Magic Mike, flamenco dancers. At one point there was a chimpanzee. Oh, geez. I'd given up drinking the night Tom and I accidentally made Lilly. Horrible decision makers like me should not be allowed near fruity alcoholic beverages.

"OK, I am sorry," I finally said.

"I lost my job over this trip, and you were a total downer the entire time."

"I said I'm sorry."

"You're not going to start crying again, are you?"

"No, but can you really blame me?"

"Yes!" Kevin jammed his pinkie into his ear and gave it a jiggle, then pulled it back to inspect his findings. "Have you seen him since you got back?"

"If you mean Tom, then no. I haven't."

"Have you talked to Chase?"

"Not about…*it*, no. I've been busy. We found a dead woman in the attic at the Burbank building."

Kevin blinked. "Why the hell didn't you lead with that?"

"Because I figured you'd want to get mad at me first."

"You're no fun to get mad at when you're agreeable. I don't like it."

"You're an idiot."

"Thank you! I like feisty Cambria way more than *my-life-is-ruined-so-I'm-going-to-cry-about-it-for-three-days-straight-and-drink-until-I-pass-out-in-a-pool-of-my-own-vomit-in-the-middle-of-a-wedding-chapel* Cambria."

"You promised to never tell that story."

"And I haven't." He jerked his head, and I stepped into his apartment. Kevin had the same floor plan I did, with the spacious living room, attached square kitchen, and little dinette area. The first time I saw his place, the walls were covered in newspaper clippings. The carpet had been ripped out and replaced with scuffed, black rubber flooring. Blue and pink swirls were spray painted on the ceiling with a disco ball mounted in the center. All the kitchen cabinet doors were missing, and there was a seventies-inspired yellow refrigerator wrapped in a heavy chain with the words *Live Explosives* written in Sharpie across the front. But that was back when he was on drugs.

Now, it looked pretty much the same, minus the refrigerator. He'd taken off the chain.

Also, he had a snake.

Viper was wrapped around a headless statue in the corner of the room. I kept my distance. I'd seen what Viper could do to a mouse, and I was not about to go near him.

Kevin's laptop was open on the coffee table, with help wanted ads on the screen.

"Looking for a new job?" I asked.

"My probation officer is breathing down my neck. Apparently, I'm not supposed to leave the state, and I need a job…blah, blah, blah. Whatever."

"What about working as a sketch artist?"

"Nah, I've given that up."

"Why? You were so good." He'd been taking classes. His ability to create a rough sketch of a suspect had come in handy on several occasions.

"Meh." He shrugged.

"You sorta need to pay rent soon." After Kevin's last stint in rehab, the McMills's trustee, Trevor, revoked the rent-free provision from Kevin's agreement. He thought it would force Kevin to grow up and accept accountability. Not so sure it did anything but build more resentment on Kevin's end.

"Are you here as my supportive friend or greedy landlord?" Kevin fell onto the couch with a grunt.

"Supportive friend…who needs support."

"You're not going to cry again, are you? Because you look like one of those Shar-Pei dogs when you cry. Trust me, it ain't pretty."

"*Thanks*, and I will not cry."

"Good. Sit." He patted the spot next to him.

I lowered onto the couch, still keeping an eye on Viper. "Did you ever visit the Burbank property when you were younger?"

"Hell, nope."

"Why not?"

"My parents never took me there because they're horrible, awful, malevolent, foolhardy, abysmal people."

"Have you been reading your thesaurus?"

"Best ten bucks I ever spent. Anyway. *Blah, blah, blah.* Hurry up. You found a dead body and…"

I blew out a breath. "Yesterday, a dead woman was found in a barrel, hidden behind a wall in the attic. They think she was killed at least twenty-five years ago, which puts her there around when Patrick took over. There are two roommates who would drag big black bags up—"

"You take *forever* to tell a story," Kevin cut me off.

The fact I'd never smacked him on the backside of the head was a miracle… *Wait a second.* A memory flashed through my mind of the two of us sitting at a bar in Vegas. He'd told the waiter I was a retired call girl, and I'd smacked him on the backside of the head. So I guess there was no miracle after all.

"I want to get my hands on the archives for the Burbank building," I said.

"You're looking at me like I can help you."

"Trevor told Patrick no, but I really need to look. Do you have any idea of how I could get my hands on those files?"

Kevin scratched his belly and smacked his lips. "Yeah, so, I could get you what you need."

"How?"

"Girl, I've got my ways."

"We can't do anything else illegal."

"I *told* you the Bellagio fountains were not a swimming pool," he said. "No, nothing illegal. Be ready first thing in the morning, and I'll take you to Trevor's office."

"I can't go in the morning because it's Lilly's first day of preschool."

He grunted. "You always play the mom card."

"It's the only card I've got."

* * *

I left Kevin's apartment feeling drained and ready for bed. The sun hung low in the sky, and the temp had cooled to an enjoyable seventy-five degrees. I could see the residents from Apartment 13 lounging by the pool. I could hear Sophie from Apartment 36 yelling at her son, Lumber, to stop drawing on the walls. I could smell the sweet spices simmering in Mr. and Mrs. Nguyen's apartment, and I could almost taste her delicious beef pho. I could feel the slight breeze on my face as I gazed up at Cedar Creek towering over us.

It was strange to think that this time next year, I could be standing at my window, staring down at this apartment complex, reminiscing of my time spent here. The residents, and the crimes, the arrests, and that one time Larry from Apartment 32 fell off the roof and tried to sue me. Then there was that one time I accidentally burned down the lobby. Chase and I had first met while I was sitting on the picnic table near the pool. He'd been working as the maintenance man at the time. I had practically combusted at the sight of him. He still had that effect on me. Which was why I dreaded the conversation we had to have.

Back at my apartment, Lilly was watching *Toy Story*, and Amy was curled up on the couch with her phone. "This is seriously the best book, Cambria. You have to read it. It's like I'm reading your life, except it's super hot, and set on a different planet. We have to meet Reena tomorrow."

"I'm planning on it."

"I think I'll buy a paperback. I want to highlight scenes in case my agent scores me an audition."

"Don't you think it's weird that Reena took off right after I talked to the old maintenance man?"

"If the maintenance man is anything like Zork, then I doubt the two still talk."

"Who the heck is Zork?"

"He's the maintenance man at Borbank. The two are having a hot fling right now, but I'm fairly certain he's hooking up with a goatshifter in Apartment 7Z."

"Right. OK. Anyway. I'll be right back."

"Where are you going?"

"Bathroom." I shut the door to my bedroom and locked it. My suitcase was still in my closet, filled with the clothes I'd taken with me on my trip. It would take me at least a week to unpack. If not longer.

I first had to remove the giant elephant, and toss the stuffed animal across the room. Then I sat on the floor, unzipped the front pouch of my suitcase, and pulled out the little blue box. Inside was a simple, gold, solitaire diamond ring. I slipped it onto my finger and watched the way the light danced off the small diamond. I could barely handle being a mother, girlfriend, friend, and apartment manager. Could I handle being a wife?

I wasn't so sure.

CHAPTER NINE

Easily adapts

Anyway. I didn't have time to dwell on any potential engagements. It was Lilly's first day of school, and dropping her off was far more emotional than I anticipated.

"Momma, why are you crying?"

"Because you're so pretty. Just one more picture."

Lilly held up her lunchbox and forced a smile. She had on the Munsters shirt with capri jeans, her hair in pigtails with big pink bows, and she sported a new pair of white Converse shoes. I took roughly two hundred pictures—stopped to erase a few because the memory on my phone was getting full—then took about two hundred more.

"Take one of Lilly and me." I thrust my phone into Amy's hands, and crouched down next to my baby girl, and smiled. The Little People Preschool was a block away from my apartment, located in a purple building with pink shutters. The teachers were friendly, and welcoming, and none of them had warrants out for their arrest, criminal hits, or evictions on their records (Tom and I did the research). It was the perfect place for Lilly, which made the three hundred dollars a week for three days a little easier to swallow.

"Daddy!" Lilly pushed me out of the way and bolted.

Tom pulled his aviators from his face, and hugged our daughter with his good arm, kissing her on the forehead.

"Why is Tom's arm in a sling?" Amy asked.

"Long story."

"Let me guess. You were with Chase, wrapped in a *hot*, passionate kiss, when Tom appeared. He grabbed Chase by the fur, a fight ensued, and the victor took you to bed."

I gave her a look.

"I'm getting way too into this book. But I'm thinking I should audition for Mcola, Zankla's best friend. I could totally play the shape-shifting werewolf. Right?"

"Totally," I said and waved to Tom. I'd been up all night imagining how this interaction would go, and the sight of him gave me an instant headache.

"Hey, Cam." Tom sauntered up, holding Lilly by the hand. "*Hello,* Amy."

"Tom," she said, giving him the once-over. "You look like crap."

"Thanks. Hey, how'd your dancing competition go?"

"I'll wait in the car and read." Amy padded to the parking lot.

"I really like razzing her," Tom said to me once Amy was out of earshot.

"And she really hates it."

"Thus, the reason I do it." He released his flirty side smirk and kissed me on the cheek. "OK, Cam, let's a take picture."

"It's Cam*bria*, and I already took around four hundred. I'll send them to you."

"I need some of her and me." He handed me his phone, and I took another hundred pictures. Seeing Tom and Lilly side-by-side reminded me how much they looked alike. It's really hard when someone you love so much looks like someone who has the ability to drive you absolutely bonkers.

About a thousand pictures later, we were ready to drop our little girl off at her very first day of preschool. As we opened the door and signed her in, the woman in the barrel came to my mind. Was the woman in the barrel a mother? Had she walked her own child to preschool? Was there a mother out there living in misery for the last twenty to thirty years, wondering where her daughter was?

These were the questions I hoped to get to the bottom of today.

Lilly darted right for the bin of blocks without so much as a "see you later" or an "I love you" or a "thank you for raising me." It killed me to think of Kevin's parents so easily dismissing their own child. You'd have to drag me away from mine. And the teacher practically did.

"She'll be fine," Ms. Nicole assured us, ushering Tom and me to the door.

"But—" I started to protest.

"She'll have a great time. We'll see you at pickup." Ms. Nicole closed and locked the door.

Tom and I pressed our faces against the window.

"How can she just leave us like that?" I asked, wiping away a tear…or two.

Fine, I was sobbing.

"I don't know," Tom said.

I looked up at him, his forehead pressed against the glass, eyes wet, and face stoic as he watched our little girl. The day I showed up on his doorstep and announced my pregnancy, he swore. He cried. He cursed. He sobbed. He got all lawyer-y on me and demanded a paternity test. Then he attached the F-word to a variety of different nouns. In that moment, I was fully prepared to raise our child on my own. Who would have thought this handsome playboy would have turned out to be a wonderful, supportive, doting father?

Tom gazed down, his eyes locked on mine—hazel on blue. I felt a familiar twinge in my stomach. I'd spent so many years pining over this man, only to have my heart broken with each rejection, each new fling he'd bring home, each time he'd profess his feelings, only to pull back seconds later. I was so busy trying not to vomit on this emotional roller coaster he was taking me on that I'd never stopped to ask myself what would happen when the ride was over. What would happen if he gave up his playboy ways and wanted to settle down with me? What would happen if he reciprocated my feelings?

I loved Tom. I knew I did. But I did not trust him. Not with my heart.

"Bye." I rushed out the door.

"Cam, wait." He grabbed my elbow and spun me around. I nearly head-butted his chest.

Do not look him in the eyes, Cambria.

Do not do it.

Nothing good happened after direct eye contact. I'd learned that lesson the hard way.

"No, Tom. I'm not rehashing anything…except, did you tell Lilly you wanted Chase to go away forever?"

"No!"

"You sure?"

"Yes, I'm sure. Why does it matter? Chase can't possibly still be around after what happened."

"Uh…I have to go."

"Hold on." He still had me by the elbow. But it's not like I was making a great effort to get away.

Note to self: Check if the new job comes with mental health benefits.

Pretty sure I needed intense therapy rather than vision.

"You told him, right?" Tom asked.

"I gotta go," I said to his chest.

"Don't run again."

"Look, I don't have time for this. I have a huge work problem that I must deal with."

"Did you not get the job at the complex next door?"

"Not yet. They're still running my background check. Which is why I need to keep a low profile, and…well…" I launched into the entire story of the woman in the barrel. Might as well. He was bound to hear about it eventually. I did so without eye contract, staring directly at his clavicle.

"How many murders do you plan to solve this year?" he asked.

"It's not my fault people keep showing up dead. What am I supposed to do?"

"Call the police, let them handle it, move on."

Sound advice, I'd give him that. "It's not just about my job. This woman is at a medical examiner's office, and who knows how long it'll be before they're able to identify her. Even with the media's help. This could take years. I already have a few leads, and I really think I can help."

Tom ran a hand through his hair. "What do you need me to do?"

Oh. I hadn't expected him to offer. I was sure I'd need legal advice at some point during my investigation. Until then… "Pick Lilly up from school."

"Got it." Tom cupped my cheek in the palm of his hand, and I directed my eyes to his chin. "I meant what I said when I gave you that ring."

"The problem is, Tom, I don't know if you meant what you said. I think you freaked out, jumped on a plane, and made a rash decision."

"It wasn't rash. I thought about it the entire plane ride over."

"It's a thirty minute flight."

"You can do a lot of thinking in thirty minutes. I meant every word I said. I do love you. I want to be together. I want to be a family. I want you in my life as more than the mother of my kid."

"I'm not doing this again, Tom. Not now." I forced my legs to move and successfully managed to walk away.

"That's fear talking. You know you can trust me, Cam," Tom called after me. "Otherwise you wouldn't have changed your mind!"

I swung open the passenger side door of my car and crawled over Amy.

"What did Tom just say?" she asked.

"Nothing." I shoved the key into the ignition, pumped the gas a few times, reattached the rearview mirror, and we were off. I checked my watch. "Do you want to come with me to run an errand with Kevin?"

"No, drop me at the bookstore. I want to grab the rest of the books in the series."

CHAPTER TEN

————

Excellent judge of character

Downtown Los Angeles smelled like BO, smog, and pot. Lots and lots of pot. I pulled the collar of my shirt over my nose to keep from getting a secondary high while I crossed the street, following Kevin. We'd parked in a lot around the block. Cost me twenty bucks for the first hour, and five dollars every thirty minutes thereafter.

Note to self: Should you not get the job at Cedar Creek, look into parking lot management.

The office building was tall and blended in with the other ten high-rises on the street. We stepped into the air-conditioned lobby with about fifteen other people, all gathered around the elevators, staring at their phones.

I clutched my bag and tried not to appear as anxious as I felt. I really, really hated elevators. And it wasn't the thought of plunging to my death, or being crammed up against strangers in a tiny box, or the possibility of being stuck in that tiny box crammed with strangers while dangling fifty feet above the ground by a thin cable, that made me nervous.

It was *all* of the above.

"You look like you're trying to hold in a fart," Kevin said, loud enough for everyone to hear.

"Leave me alone," I muttered through a smile.

The elevator doors parted, and everyone pushed forward. I ended up face-to-face with a woman who had breakfast stuck between her front teeth. We avoided eye contact as the doors closed. I instantly ran through all the worst-case scenarios. *Cable breaks. Earthquake hits. Fire. Flood. Medical emergency. Elevator stalls.* The good news was, if we were to get stuck, I had a package of fish crackers in my purse, along with an orange juice box, two chocolate chip cookies, and a water bottle I could empty should anyone need to relieve themselves.

Note to self: You're neurotic.

Up to the second floor we went. The elevator dinged and paused for a little too long.

Breathe. Breathe. Breathe. Breathe. Breathe.

The doors finally parted, and I practically leapt out into the hallway.

"Were you even listening to me?" Kevin asked.

"Huh?"

"I was talking to you the entire time. Telling you our plan."

"Oh, sorry. I was preoccupied. What's the plan?"

"OK, we're going to walk in."

"Right."

"And we're going to say hi to the receptionist."

"Got it."

"We're going to ask for Trevor."

"OK."

"Then we're going to ask Trevor if we can look at the archives."

My shoulders dropped. "Are you kidding me? Patrick told me Trevor said no."

"I can be very persuasive." He wiggled his hips in a circle.

"Trevor is your cousin."

"I know. Get your head out of the gutter."

Oh, geez.

The lobby of Trevor's office looked exactly as I pictured it would: bamboo trees, Buddha statues, no chairs—only overstuffed pillows, crystals (lots and lots of crystals), oil diffusers, and some sort of bell/guitar/flute melody playing in the background. Felt like I'd just stepped into a day spa, not the office of a man who managed millions and millions and *millions* of dollars' worth of real estate. While some might find his ways unprofessional, I found them refreshing.

The receptionist had more piercings in her face than I could count, and she brought her hands together and bowed. So I bowed back.

"Trevor in?" Kevin picked at his back teeth. "I'm Kevin *McMills*."

"Did I hear Kevin?" Trevor stepped from behind a sheer folding partition. Trevor typically wore flannel shirts rolled up to his elbows to better show off the stack of rope bracelets tied around his hairy wrists. But today he had on a long white tunic. His dark hair was twisted into a bun on the top of his head. His beard was big and poufy and looked like pubic hair. His glasses were dark-rimmed and about two sizes too big for his face. "What are you doing here—oh!" Trevor's eyes landed on me. "You brought my favorite manager."

I forgot what a close talker Trevor was. I also forgot how much he liked to hug, and that he was one of those kiss-on-the-cheek greeters.

For the record: I am none of the above.

Which made our reunion slightly uncomfortable.

"I heard about the poor dead soul at Burbank." Trevor had my face squished between his hands, forcing my lips to pucker. "I told Patrick many times there was a disturbance there. Now I know why."

"Who told you?" I asked through my fish lips.

Trevor released my face but remained a solid three inches from my nose. I went cross-eyed looking at him. "A detective named Hampton arrived this morning. Here. Come into my office." Trevor draped his arm around my shoulders. "You, too, Kevin."

Kevin muttered under his breath. Something about this is what happens when they legalize pot.

Trevor's office was really just a big open space with yoga mats, statues, crystals, and a laptop on the floor near a beanbag.

I sat on an overstuffed blue pillow, while Kevin opted to stand. Trevor crossed the room, opened a drawer, and returned holding some sort of branch. "This will help you, cousin." Trevor lit the end of the branch on fire and made circles of smoke around Kevin's head. "Take deep breaths."

Kevin could not have looked more unimpressed if he'd tried.

"What does that do?" I asked.

"It rids negative energy, generates wisdom and clarity, and promotes healing."

"I'm next." Not that I believed in all that...that much. But at this point, I was up for anything. Especially clarity.

Wisdom wouldn't hurt either.

Trevor circled the burning branch around my head. I didn't feel any different. It must take a while to work.

Trevor put his burning stick away and sank into his beanbag. "Are you here because you took me up on my offer?" he asked Kevin.

Offer?

"No. I'm not a nutjob like you," he said. "What we want is to look at the archives from the Burbank building. Cambria thinks she might know who killed the chick who croaked in the attic."

Kevin wasn't kidding when he gave me his plan.

"You think you've figured it out who the killer was? Or who the woman was?" Trevor asked.

"The killer. Alvin and Sherman lived in Apartment 2B right around when this woman died. I'd like to look at their file."

"Of course you can," Trevor said. "Absolutely."

I almost fell off my pillow. "B-but you said no."

"No, I said yes."

"No, you said *no*."

Trevor stroked his beard. "I think we are having two different conversations. Connect with me." He put his forehead against mine. "Tell me what it is you're saying."

I became suddenly conscious of my breath. "When Patrick asked if I could look at the archived files, he said you said no."

"Why would I say no? The only point of keeping the files is so we can reference them at a later date if needed. Sounds like we *need* them now."

"What did you say to Patrick, then?" I asked, trying to understand.

"I said yes, of course. Sadly, I don't know who this woman could have been. All I know is that she had a beautiful spirit."

"I call bull," Kevin blurted out.

A flash of annoyance crossed Trevor's face. Then, as if making some sort of inner resolution, he wiggled his shoulders and smiled. "I am sensitive to people's auras. I knew there was a disturbance at the building. But I also knew there was a beautiful, protective spirit there."

Kevin might call this bull, but I believed Trevor. The first time I met him, he talked about the disturbance at the Burbank building. It's one of the reasons he fired the previous manager and hired me. Not to brag, but I had a blue aura.

Whatever that meant

"I'll get the key for you," Trevor said.

"Hold on." I grabbed Trevor by the wrist. "You told Patrick *yes*?"

"Correct."

"Do the McMillses know about the barrel?"

"I've left a message for my aunt and uncle. I expect to hear from them shortly."

I shook my head, trying desperately to understand without jumping to the worst-case scenario. Why would Patrick lie to me?

Answer: He's guilty.

No. I pushed the thought out of my head as quickly as it entered. Trevor might have been sensitive to spirits and auras and all that. But I knew people. People like Patrick. He was a good man and would never kill anyone. If he did, he certainly wouldn't store anyone in the attic of the Burbank building.

"Sounds like Patrick has something to hide," Kevin said.

"No!" I snapped. "He's just been…busy. That's all. There must have been a misunderstanding." I hoped.

"There's something fishy going on," Kevin said. "That's all I'm saying."

I felt like saying *no duh, there's a dead body. Of course there's something fishy.* But *duh* is not a very intelligent response, and Trevor was still my boss's boss.

"How long have you been the trustee?" I asked Trevor, ignoring Kevin, who was now nudging me with his toe, wanting me to hurry. But this was important.

"The trust was formed in 1996. It was the year I graduated law school."

"And you didn't know about the barrels in the attic?"

"Of course I did. As soon as I was told that I'd be managing the trust, I did a complete tour of all the properties in the portfolio. My uncle has a hard time letting go of things. I took it upon myself to clear out the attic, and I can assure you there wasn't a body in any of the barrels."

"*You* moved all the barrels?"

"Yes, I did. They were a beast to get down the stairs into the apartment. I was in much better shape back then."

"What stairs?" I asked.

"There were pull-down stairs in Apartment 2B, but I broke them when I took down the barrels."

A thought skyrocketed into my brain. "How many barrels did you move?"

"Four."

"Four?"

"Four."

"Four?"

"Four."

"Are you sure there were four?"

"Yes, Cambria, I moved them personally. They were big and awkward, and I nearly killed myself lowering them down the stairs. There were four."

"Aha!"

Trevor scratched his head. "What does *aha* mean?"

"Uh..." May and Neo had both said there were five barrels. I'd counted five rings. Trevor just admitted to moving four of them. Which meant one was missing. The one with the woman. The one hidden behind the wall. Which meant she did in fact die around the time Alvin and Sherman moved out, Patrick was hired, and Kevin was sent away.

Except, I didn't tell Trevor any of this. For all I knew, he put the woman in the barrel. It seemed unlikely, given that he was in his early twenties and she was in her mid-to-late thirties. What would have been their connection? But you never knew. So instead I said, "Aha! I'm so happy to be here!"

Which prompted Trevor to wave his burning stick over my head a few more times.

* * *

Could be because I spent way too much time watching crime shows, but I'd pictured this going down a lot differently. I'd imagined Kevin having to create a distraction while I broke into a closet, used my phone as a flashlight, tried to grab as many files as I could, and stuffed them under my shirt before I was discovered.

I did not anticipate Trevor handing over a key. Which was precisely what happened. Trevor gave Kevin and me a key to an office suite two doors down, wished us luck, and rubbed oil on our foreheads.

"What offer was Trevor talking about?" I asked Kevin as we walked down the hallway.

"He wants me to work for him."

"What? Why don't you? That's a brilliant idea."

"I don't want anything to do with him or my parents. You heard Trevor. My dad doesn't get rid of anything. He's a hoarder. But he had no problem getting rid of me. As soon as they kicked me out, they immediately took Trevor in. And he's a complete nutjob! Always has been. They never even gave him the time of day. Then suddenly they were like *'hey, want to be a millionaire?'* I'm not even sure they hate me because I'm gay. I think they just suck at being people. You know how you overly baby your kid?"

"I do not." OK, maybe a little. But that's only because she's my baby. "Anyway. Continue."

"My mom barely acknowledged my existence. My dad was better, but not much. There weren't bedtime stories, or sparkle toast, or any sort of physical affection. On my first day of school, my mom dropped me at the curb."

"That's terrible, Kevin." And yet explained so much of his personality. "I'm so sorry."

"Yeah, whatever. Don't get all sappy. It's unattractive." Kevin stopped at Suite 223. "You ready for this?"

"For what?"

He pushed open the door.

I exclaimed, "Holy hell. Where are we?"

"This was my mom and dad's office. Like Trevor said, Ernest McMills doesn't get rid of anything. Looks exactly the same as the last time I was here."

No, he didn't. It was like stepping into an episode of *Extreme Hoarders, Office Space Edition.*

Boxes. Boxes everywhere. Boxes on what was once a receptionist desk. The old-style phone was still there, next to a typewriter. Boxes on the floor. Boxes by a large copier machine. Boxes and boxes and boxes and boxes.

"There's no way we're going to find anything in here," I said.

"Probably not."

I took the lid off a file box and quickly determined it was filled with zoning permits. "Does being in here bring back a lot of emotions?" I asked.

"No."

"I don't believe you for a second. This has to be hard."

"Then why are you asking?"

"So we can talk about it."

Kevin exhaled a telling sigh. "I've been kissed on the cheek by the whack-a-doodle my parents let run their fortune, been covered in oil, and I smell like"—he took a whiff of his sleeve—"what was that burning twig thing?"

"Not sure."

"Smells like pot."

"My guess is sage."

"Whatever. Stop talking and start looking."

Fine.

It took about an hour before we located a group of boxes filled with Burbank's archived residential files. They were in the bathroom, behind the door, being used as a makeshift table to keep air freshener and extra rolls of toilet paper on.

I sat down and flipped through each file until I found Apartment 2B. Turned out Alvin's last name was Leo, and Sherman's was Varner. There were copies of their social security cards, bank statements, also birth dates and all sorts of personal information. Leo had long brown hair, crooked teeth, and thin eyebrows. Sherman had small facial features and a long neck. "This is fantastic."

"You sure these guys had something do with the dead woman?" Kevin asked.

"At this point, I don't know. They moved out right around when the woman died. They could have emptied one of the barrels, put the body in, and left." I took pictures of all of Alvin's and Sherman's information, and I sent it to Chase. Then I called Tom.

"Missed me?" he answered.

"No. Remember when you asked what you could do to help with my investigation?"

"Yes, and you said I could pick up Lilly."

"Right. One more thing. Can you run a background check and look for criminal hits on two people for me? I'll text you all the information."

"I'll do anything for you, Cam."

"Great. Can you please stop calling me Cam, then?"

"Anything but that. Send me the info, and I'll see what I can find."

We hung up, and I set the file aside.

"I still don't understand how you got two hot guys after you," Kevin said. "I got no hot guys after me. This really isn't fair."

"Trust me, it's not as fun as it sounds." At all.

I continued to search through the files, opening each one, scanning the pictures, and reading through the notes. Until I got to Apartment 11A. "Look at this. Apartment 11A had a series of women from El Salvador moving in and out. They all listed Burbank Flowers as their place of employment."

"So?"

"*So*, the woman in the barrel was Hispanic."

"That narrows it down to pretty much everyone."

"Just listen to me. All these women were Hispanic. According to their visas, most of them were petite, and all of them had brown hair."

"But they lived there in the seventies and eighties. I thought the lady was killed in the nineties?"

"No, some of these women lived there in the early-to-mid nineties." I licked my finger and flipped through each page of the thick file. "There were ten roommates within the time frame. Which meant they crossed Alvin's and Sherman's paths. None of these women have move-out sheets, which is weird."

"You think one of these ten chicks could be the corpse?"

"I think it's possible one of these *women* could be the *victim.*"

"When you get all politically correct, it makes me want to barf. What now?"

"We'll go to Burbank Flowers."

"Don't you have to do your actual job today?"

Right.

CHAPTER ELEVEN

Reliable

I called in sick.

Well, I *emailed* in sick. Patrick still wasn't answering the phone. I didn't have much work to do anyway, and any resident in need could reach me on my cell or through the emergency line.

Burbank Flowers was busy for a Wednesday afternoon. So much so, I had to stop and think if there was a holiday I was forgetting. Then I saw the *Going out of Business* sign above the cash register. *Everything half off.*

I approached the counter. A short woman in her late forties–early fifties with a long dark braid was shoving roses into a vase. I rang the *Ring for Service* bell to get her attention.

"Hi, this may seem odd," I said, once she turned around. "I'm an apartment manager here in Burbank, and years ago, several women from El Salvador both lived at my building and worked here. I'm trying to find information on them."

"What apartment building?" The woman had a faint accent.

I gave her the address, and her face lit with recognition.

"I used to live there," she said. "Back when I first moved here from El Salvador in 1978."

"Do you know if any of the roommates who lived in that apartment happened to disappear?"

Maria gave me the once-over, her brow furrowed.

"We ain't cops," Kevin added. "She's just intrusive. That means nosey. Found it in my thesaurus."

"Thank you, Kevin," I said. "Anyway. Did any of the roommates happen to disappear? Or hang out with two men who lived upstairs—Alvin and Sherman."

"I vaguely remember Alvin and Sherman. They used to have parties, right?"

"So I've heard."

"No one disappeared when I lived there."

"Did anyone happen to have dentures?"

"I don't think so. We came from a small village in El Salvador, and we didn't have access to dental there. I know a few of us had missing teeth. I got an implant last year." She smiled. I had no idea which tooth was fake. She had a good dentist.

"Did you personally know all the roommates?"

"We were all cousins or close family friends. Originally, my cousin Dominique moved there and rented the apartment. I came and moved in with her, and then Angelica came. And it worked like that for years. One person moved out—another came over from El Salvador."

"And everyone is still alive and well?"

"I don't keep up with everyone anymore. My cousin Angela does."

Angela? The name sounded familiar. "And Angela is alive?" I asked.

"She lives in North Carolina."

I'd taken pictures of the ten woman who fit in our time frame, and I scrolled through them until I found Angela's. Two down. Eight to go. This very well could have been a pointless endeavor. But most of these were petite Hispanic women with dark hair, and no move-out information. Where was the deposit and move-out reconciliation sent? Legally, we had to reconcile every move out. Even if the resident wasn't entitled to a refund of their deposit. If we didn't have a forwarding address, we had to send it to the apartment they'd just moved from in case there was a forwarding address at the post office. You couldn't just leave it alone. It was illegal.

Maria gave me Angela's number, and I sent her a text message, asking her to call me. Before we left, Maria looked through all the pictures on my phone, and I was able to delete more women who she was positive were still alive. When she asked why I was looking for them, I didn't have a choice but to tell her the truth.

Maria slapped a hand over her mouth. "And you think it was one of my cousins?"

"Honestly, I have no idea. I'm trying to identify everyone who lived there who fit the description and was there in the midnineties."

Maria grabbed the edge of the counter. "Then you have to speak to Angela. She is the family busybody and keeps tabs on everyone. I'll send her a text as well, to make sure she calls you."

"Thank you." I felt bad worrying Maria. This could turn out to be nothing. Or it could turn out to be everything. The problem was, I wouldn't know until I confirmed every woman who lived in Apartment 11A was still alive.

Kevin and I left after Maria and I exchanged information. There was a total of six women from Apartment 11A still on my phone, and I sent all their pictures to Chase, hoping he'd be able to verify their whereabouts.

Then, my phone rang. It was Tom.

"What's wrong?" I stepped out of the flower shop and slipped on my sunglasses. "Is it Lilly? Please tell me it isn't Lilly. Is she hurt? What happened?

"Nothing," Tom said. "Calm down. I called about your two guys."

Oh. That. *Phew.* "What do you know?"

"From what I can tell, Alvin is still a set designer. No criminal hits aside from a few moving violations. Sherman, on the other hand, he has assault with a deadly weapon. Domestic abuse charges. Drug charges. Let me put it this way—his rap sheet is ten pages long."

"Does he have a current address?"

"Yes, it's 3600 Guard Way in Lompoc, California."

I repeated the address out loud for Kevin so he could look it up. "Where is Lompoc?" I asked Tom. "Is that in the Valley?"

Kevin tapped my shoulder and showed me his phone.

Oh, come on. "It's a prison, Tom. Why didn't you just say *he's in prison…* Are you laughing at me?"

"No, I'm laughing with you."

"I'm not laughing."

"Do you honestly think I would give you the home address of a man who has a violent criminal history?"

"No?"

"He's five years into a twenty-year sentence," Tom said. "This is probably your guy."

"I've narrowed the victim's identity down to six immigrants from El Salvador who all match the description of the woman in the barrel, and they lived there around the time when she was killed."

"Cool. Case solved. Will you marry me now?"

"Goodbye." I hung up the phone and pinched the bridge of my nose.

"Can we go home?" Kevin asked. "I need to find a job, and I'm hungry."

"I still think you should take Trevor up on his offer."

"He only made the offer because he took some coo-coo-head meditation course about mending fences, and balancing family, and blah…blah…blah. He feels guilty because he has my inheritance. Instead of giving me a job, he could make my rent free again."

"But isn't having a job better?"

"No!"

"You could learn all about property management."

"I grew up in the business. I know everything there is to know about the industry."

"Then why do you constantly break the rules?"

"Knowing the right and doing the right are two different things."

Ain't that the truth.

* * *

When I got home, Amy was curled up on the couch reading. The blinds were drawn, and an açai bowl from the health food mart down the street was on the floor, untouched.

I liked Clean Amy better than Bookworm Amy.

"How'd you get here?" I asked.

"Uber. Your office phone has been ringing off the hook," she said, not lifting her eyes from the book.

"What are you reading?" Kevin asked.

"The first Zankla book. Ever heard of the series?"

Kevin bent over in a laughing fit, slapping his knee and gasping for breath.

"Is that a yes?" I asked.

"That's the former manager chick." He ran a finger under his eyes, catching the tears, still laughing. "It's supposed to be about her time working at Burbank. Let me read that when you're done."

"Mmmhmm," Amy said, not exactly paying attention.

I went to my office and checked the messages. Three were from Silvia, still trying to confirm our double date on Friday, and to let me know Larry, her neighbor, was on his patio shirtless. I had a message from Fox, wanting to talk about his goats. There was one message from Marlene in Apartment 11A at Burbank, wanting to talk about her neighbor. Nothing from Patrick.

Great.

I dropped my face into my hands. Patrick was making it very difficult to not suspect him of murder. But then, it was *Patrick*. I remembered the day he'd offered me this job. I had locked myself in the bathroom of the crap-hole apartment I'd been living in at the time. When he told me the job was mine, I'd practically passed out from excitement. We'd been through so much together over the last ten months: a drug problem, murder, fire, murder, fire, and that time Larry fell from the roof. I'd never had a hard time getting ahold of Patrick. I managed his flagship property. He took my calls.

Unless… I sat up straighter. Was he ghosting me? Had he spoken to the Dashwoods already and he was so upset that he couldn't talk to me? I wasn't sure how Dr. Dashwood managed to get ahold of him. I'd given them his cell number, and his phone was off and went straight to a full voice mail box.

Ugh. I hated not knowing what was going on. I wrestled with dropping everything and going to look for Patrick, and staying put to do my job.

Ultimately, I went with the latter.

I looked up Alvin Leo on Facebook. He was easy enough to find. Alvin now had a goatee, shaggy white hair, and diamond earrings. I sent him a message with my phone number, asking him to please call me.

Then, I called Marlene. She answered on the first ring. "Cambria, we have a big problem. I can hear someone being tortured."

Tortured? "What happened?" I asked.

"I heard a woman screaming upstairs. It might be coming from the attic. I heard the police found something suspicious up there yesterday."

Yes, they had. They found a dead woman, not a screaming one. Of course, I didn't say this to her. "Did you call the police?"

"No, I didn't. Should I call them?"

"If you believe someone is in danger, then you should absolutely…" A thought came to my mind. "Hold on one second." I put Marlene on hold and called Fox using my office phone. As soon as he picked up, I could hear the goats screaming in the background. "Fox, I'm getting complaints from residents about the goats."

"It's not my fault," he said. "They're not happy."

"They would probably be happier if they weren't cooped up in an apartment. Have you made any progress in finding them a home?"

"No. I was able to download a certificate off the internet to make them emotional support animals, though."

Ugh. This was a muddled area of property management. Legally, residents were allowed to have emotional support pets, so long as they provided proof that said animal was for therapeutic purposes. Legally, I wasn't allowed to ask what the therapeutic purpose was. Illegally, the residents could print off a fake certificate online stating that these animals were for therapy. Legally, I couldn't ask if the certificate was fake. Nor could I charge a pet deposit.

I was completely sympathetic to those who did need an emotional animal. Hell, if I weren't allergic to everything with fur, I'd have been first in line to get one. I was an emotional wreck.

However, Fox just openly admitted to printing a certificate online, and I felt comfortable enough that any judge—

should Fox sue for discrimination—would see that accidentally buying two goats wasn't good for anyone's mental health. Including Fox's. Being that he'd yelled at them to stop screaming at least three times since he'd picked up the phone.

"Fox, if you don't remove the goats, then I'm going to have to serve you with a notice to vacate."

"My *lawyer* said I could keep them."

"Great. What's your lawyer's name and number? I'll have him speak to mine."

"Uh…his name i-is…," Fox mumbled something under his breath. I'd called his bluff, and he knew it. Residents threw around the "lawyer" word like it was candy. I had serious doubt Fox had an attorney on retainer on the off chance he'd accidentally buy two goats. "I'll figure something out."

"Soon." I hung up and returned to Marlene. "I'm so sorry to keep you waiting. You'll be happy to know that no one was being tortured. The screaming was coming from a resident who has goats in his apartment. They are not allowed to be there, and he will be getting rid of them shortly."

"That's…*weird.*"

Agreed. "Is there anything else I can do for you?"

"No. I guess not." There was a brief pause. "You sure it was goats?"

"I am. Please feel free to call me if the problem continues." We hung up, and I called Patrick. Again, he didn't answer. The call went straight to a full voice mail. I wanted to groan out loud, to throw something, or to bang my head against the desk. I was so sick of hearing: "The voice mail box is full. Good-bye."

That's it!

* * *

I'd never been to Patrick's office before. His address was displayed on my direct deposit stubs, and I pulled up the directions on my phone and said a quick prayer of thanks to the traffic gods that my ETA was only eighteen minutes. My car grumbled to life, and I was on my way. Neither Kevin nor Amy asked where I was going, how long I'd be gone, or why I was limping (I'd rammed my knee into the side of the desk in my rush to leave). They were far too invested in their Zankla books to care about murderous matters.

Elder Property Management was located in a pale building across the street from a Trader Joe's. Much to my surprise, there was a *free* parking lot designated for the small industrial park.

There were few things that made me happier than free parking.

Up on the second floor in Unit 293, I found a tinted door with Elder Property Management engraved on a brass plate. I yanked and pushed on the handle a few times with no luck. The door was locked, despite the *Hours of Operation 9AM-5PM M-F* decal on the window. I kept pushing and pulling anyway, hoping the door would magically open and there would be Patrick, sitting behind his desk, already on the phone with Hampton, assuring him that he had nothing to do with any women in barrels.

I cupped my hands around my eyes and pressed my forehead against the window. The blinds were partially drawn, and all I caught was the edge of a desk. I crouched down to get a better look. From this angle, I saw the backside of a computer and a hand on the mouse. Patrick was in there!

Or at least someone was.

I knocked on the door politely at first. When that didn't work, I used the inside of my fists until I heard the *click* of the lock. Patrick opened the door with his eyebrows raised high on his forehead. He had on a blue, collared shirt tucked into a pair of khaki pants and stark white Nike shoes on his feet. His attire often reminded me of Forest Gump's, minus the Bubba Gump hat. Patrick had a cul-de-sac of hair and a no-nonsense air to him.

"Cambria," he said. "I thought you were sick today."

So he had read my email. Just hadn't bothered to reply.

"I'm feeling better." I wanted to come right out and ask him why he'd been acting so suspicious these last two days, but decided to ease into the accusations. "Did you talk to Chase or Hampton?"

"Detective Hampton and I have been playing phone tag."

"I tried your office line, and it was disconnected."

"Everyone calls me on my cell. There was no point in paying for a line I don't use."

"Oh. OK" was all I could think to say. I clasped my hands and waited, thinking he'd invite me in. But all he did was stand there, wedged between the door and frame, staring down at me as if I'd just crashed a party I wasn't invited to. "Is that why your voice mail box is full?" I asked.

"I underestimated how many phone calls I receive a day."

Kind of hard to know how many calls you get when your phone is off was what I wanted to say. But I convinced myself to remain composed.

"Speaking of phone calls," Patrick said. "I had an interesting conversation with the Dashwoods."

Crap.

"You interviewed for a job next door," he said.

My lips were numb, and I forced words out. "Yes?"

"Is that a question or an answer?"

"Answer?"

"Why didn't you tell me you were looking for a new job?"

"They asked me if I would interview. I wasn't looking."

"I told them you'd do a great job."

My heart lifted. "Thank you, Patrick. I really appreciate it. I've loved working here, and I'm so grateful for all that you've done."

"My pleasure. Your leaving has made my decision easier."

"What decision?"

"I'm finally quitting the business."

"What? Why?" My mind went to the woman in the barrel. Maybe Patrick was the killer after all, and his guilty conscious had him making hasty decisions. He wasn't even old enough to retire!

"This business is exhausting, and now we have another murder. Do you know how much paperwork is involved every time you find a dead body?"

"Actually, Fox found the body."

"It doesn't matter. I'll let Trevor know tomorrow, and he'll hire a new management company."

"What will happen to Mr. Nguyen?"

"He's a good employee. I'm sure he'll find another job, just like you did."

My throat clenched, and I made a strangled sound. The thing was, I didn't have a new job, *yet*. There was still this murder business to deal with, and who knew if the story would get out in the news? Who knew if the Dashwoods had a more qualified applicant?

This wasn't even about *my* job. What about Mr. Nguyen? Not only would we both be unemployed, but also we'd be out of a place to live.

"Patrick, what if I stay?" My voice sounded high and shaky, and I was, I knew, seconds away from actually starting to cry. "Would you reconsider quitting?"

"I'm sick of this business, Cambria. The decision has already been made." He opened the door wider, revealing moving boxes stacked up against the wall. "I had planned to move to a home office, but I think it's time I move on."

I stepped back and bumped into a woman pushing a stroller.

"Watch where you're going," the mother said and maneuvered around me.

"W-w-w-w..." It was like my mouth had forgotten how to make words and my lips suddenly felt about ten sizes too big for my face. "You can't just quit!"

"Yes, I can." Patrick's tone was not unsympathetic. Which didn't help matters.

"B-b-but. Why did you tell me that Trevor said I couldn't look through the archived files?" I knew how accusing I sounded, but I couldn't help myself.

Patrick jammed his hands into his pockets, but he offered no words.

"Did you have something to do with the woman in the barrel?" I figured I might as well come right out and ask. It wasn't like he could fire me at this point. He was already closing up shop!

"No, I did not," he said, but I wasn't sure if I believed him or not. "I do have a lot of work to get done, and I would appreciate it if you didn't tell anyone else about this until I've had the chance."

"OK," I said, shaking my head, feeling utterly disappointed. I thought we had a good enough working relationship. Hell, we were even Facebook friends! I couldn't believe he'd quit and leave his employees high and dry. It seemed like an odd time to make such a drastic decision.

Too odd.

CHAPTER TWELVE

Vast experience in dealing with hopeless situations

I drove home, listening to Semisonic's "Closing Time" on repeat. Chances were a new management company would bring in their own staff. That's what had happened to former maintenance guy, Neo. Why wouldn't it happen to us? I never thought interviewing at Cedar Creek would mean Mr. Nguyen would lose his job, too. If I had known, then I wouldn't have done it. Mr. and Mrs. Nguyen were family.

It wasn't quite four o'clock when I pulled into my carport. I somberly walked along the pathway to my apartment, dragging my feet and feeling like someone had just dropped a fifty-pound weight on my shoulders. I opened the door to my apartment to find Amy and Kevin in the exact same positions I'd left them in. I didn't even bother saying hello and shuffled straight to my office.

I plopped into my chair, crossed my forearms on the desk, and rested my forehead against them. For a while, I concentrated on pulling air into my lungs, inhaling the lavender scent of my soap. What a giant mess.

My phone pinged. It was my mother, wanting to know how Lilly's first day of preschool went. I imagined she was sitting at her desk at work, counting down the minutes. When I didn't immediately reply, she sent another text message:

What's wrong?

I began to craft a reply when a text from Tom came in. It was a picture of Lilly standing in front of his car holding a finger painting. She was missing a bow, her hair was a mess, and there was paint on her shirt, and grass stains on her knees. But she'd never looked happier. I felt a swell in my heart. My kid was happy. At least I was doing one thing right.

I forwarded the picture to my mother, and she replied back with seven hearts. I imagined her setting the picture as her phone's background, just as I was doing.

"Is that Lilly?" Amy asked, looking over my shoulder. "What happened to her?"

"She had fun. Why aren't you with your book?"

"I finished. Kevin's reading it now. I *have* to be in this movie. It's going to be a massive hit."

"Maybe I should write a book about my job."

"Can I play you in the movie?"

"Sure."

"Good." Amy rolled up the other office chair and plopped down, crossing her legs in a slow, exaggerated movement, like a therapist preparing for an intense session. "I'm ready to hear all about New York now."

"I'm not ready to talk about it." I started organizing the drawer again.

Amy tapped her nails on the armrest in slow, rhythmic motions. "I found the ring in your suitcase."

Crud. "What were you doing in my suitcase?"

"Looking for your hair straighter."

Oh. Shoot. Served me right for not unpacking. "What did the ring look like?" I asked, trying to sound nonchalant.

"Like a beautiful one carat, white gold, vintage, halo-style, channel-set, round diamond engagement ring," she said. "Now dish. Who proposed?"

I returned my forehead to the desktop. "Chase," I said, my voice low. Which was true. The engagement ring she found was the one Chase gave me.

Amy made a strangled sound, and I turned my head to make sure she was still breathing. Her mouth was open so wide I could practically see her tonsils. "You two haven't even been together a year. Why would he propose?"

"I don't know. We hadn't talked about marriage, per se. He's been waiting for his FBI training orders, and I think he's scared I won't wait for him."

"What did you say?"

"Yes."

Amy jumped up, sending her chair crashing into the shredder and knocking it over. "She said yes!"

"Shut up!" Kevin hollered from the living room couch. "I'm reading."

"This is amazing." Amy started pacing. She did this when she was either stressed or sick or drunk or excited. I assumed it was the latter. "We'll do two bridal showers. One here, and one back home in Fresno. Bachelorette party in Cabo. I'll pick out the bridesmaid dresses, of course. I'm thinking a low cut with a high slit, black. And we're going to need to pluck your eyebrows."

"Slow your roll." I stood in her pacing path. "There's more to the story."

"Oh, no, you ruined it, didn't you? Why, Cambria? Wwwhhhhyyyy?" She perched her bony little butt up on my desk. "Wait, no. No. Tom ruined this. How many times have I told you that man does not love you? He does not want to be with you. This whole song and dance about loving you is because he hates the idea of another man in Lilly's life. Period. Please, please, tell me you didn't allow him to ruin the healthiest relationship you've ever had."

"No, he didn't…necessarily."

"So that would be a *yes*."

"No, I can ruin things all on my own," I said indignantly. "Plus I can't just go around marrying people, Amy. This is a big decision, and it's not just me. I have to consider what is best for Lilly."

"What is best for Lilly is what is best for *you*. If you're in a miserable relationship with Tom, then she's going to grow up to have a miserable relationship as well. Look at you."

"What's that supposed to mean?"

"Your parents got pregnant, decided to get married, had a horrible relationship, which totally screwed you up, and they ended up divorced. Now you have a stepmother who you hate and a mother who is slightly obsessive."

"I am not screwed up." OK, maybe I was. Crap.

The thought of Lilly having this exact conversation with her best friend in twenty-five years gave me indigestion. Or maybe it was the alarming amount of carbs I'd consumed that day.

Either way, I pulled open my drawer and grabbed my bottle of Tums. It was empty. Dang it.

Note to self: Go to Costco and buy a new case of Tums, ASAP.

Instead, I grabbed the Advil bottle and shook two into my palm. I swore the new employment package for any job in this industry should say, "Welcome to the world of property management. I hope you like ibuprofen."

"Cambria." Amy put her hands on my shoulders and looked me straight in the eyes. "I watched you pine over Tom for years, and I watched your heart break when he didn't reciprocate the feelings. Chase loves *you.*"

"I know." And after everything I'd put him through, I had no idea why. "I love him, too."

"Then marry *him.* Because we all know Tom will never get down on one knee."

Technically, she was right. "I don't know what is happening with Lilly and Chase, though."

"You and I both know Tom put ideas into her head."

"He said he didn't."

"I don't believe him for a second."

"Tom is many things, but he isn't a liar."

My phone rang. A number I didn't recognize flashed on the screen, and I answered. "This is Cambria."

Amy put her finger under my chin and forced me to look at her. "We'll resume when you're done," she said and stalked back into my apartment, closing the door behind her. I knew her well enough to know she was already on Pinterest looking up bridal schemes.

"Cambria, it's Marlene. I know you said the screaming was goats, but I just saw a woman running out of Apartment 14B. Isn't that place empty?"

"Yes, it is." I wracked my brain, trying to remember if I'd locked the door this morning. Typically, I'd leave the vacant units unlocked with applications on the kitchen counter. The building was small, traffic was light, and there was no point in me sitting there all day waiting for a prospect to pop in. But

Apartment 14B wasn't ready to show. Not with the crusty oven. I hadn't even scheduled the cleaning yet—I'd been so preoccupied with the barrel. For the life of me, I couldn't remember if I'd locked the door or not. I was sure that I'd left the fan in there. Shoot.

"I'll be right there," I told Marlene.

* * *

I called Chase, asking him to meet me at the Burbank building, and we arrived at the same time. Parking was nonexistent on the apartment-lined street. I deemed this an emergency, double parked my car, and turned on the hazard lights. Chase didn't need hazards. He had a flashing red and blue mount grill light on the driver's side roof.

I'd asked for one for Valentine's Day.

He gave me flowers instead.

Whatever.

Chase greeted me with a quick peck on the lips. "Before you ask, I haven't looked at the information you texted me. This isn't the only case I have going right now, and it's been a crazy day."

"You need to look at the info, pronto. One of the former residents in an attic access apartment has a violent criminal history."

"How'd you find this out?"

"Tom ran a background check."

Chase always tensed a little at the mention of Tom's name but never said anything. At the end of the day, Tom was part of the package. Chase knew this. It's what happens when you date a single mother.

Chase and I stepped into the courtyard. Marlene was waiting outside her apartment, biting at her nails. When she saw me approaching, she dropped her hand and ran over. "The woman was up in there screaming." She pointed to Apartment 14B.

"You sure it wasn't the goats?" I asked.

As if they heard us talking about them, the goats let out a scream, followed by Fox telling them to "shut the hell up!"

"I'm positive," Marlene said.

"Was she with anyone else?" Chase asked.

"Not that I could see."

Chase went up the stairs to Apartment 14B, and I stayed with Marlene. She hugged her waist, looking pale. "I'm freaked out about what I overheard Fox say yesterday before the goats chased me away. Was there a dead body in the attic? Is that what the police found?"

I hesitated. Only because I knew how fast rumors spread through communities. By this time tomorrow, instead of one dead woman in a barrel, it would be a triple homicide with a serial killer on the loose.

But I didn't want to lie to Marlene. Not when she appeared so upset. "Yes," I said. "Unbeknownst to any of us, the victim had been up there for many years. You don't have to worry about your safety. It was an isolated incident, a heinous crime likely committed by someone the victim knew personally."

Marlene twisted her mouth to the side and peered first up at Apartment 14B, then back at me. She did this several times. I suspected she was about to tell me she was moving, or she was going to ask for a discount on her rent since she'd been living under a corpse.

Instead, she cleared her throat and said, "I think my apartment is haunted."

Oh. Well. Didn't see that one coming.

"I know it sounds crazy," she said. "Sometimes the lights just turn on. One time I saw a woman at the foot of my bed just staring at me."

Uh…OK. "Did you ask her to leave?"

"No." Marlene lowered her voice. "She was a ghost. It was freaky as hell."

I bet.

"What did the ghost look like?" I asked.

"She was young, with dark hair."

"Did she have all her teeth?"

Marlene gave me a look, as if my question were ridiculous. Even though we were currently talking about a creeper ghost watching her sleep. "I didn't look."

Here's the thing. I didn't believe in all that paranormal, evil spirits, curses, and ghost stories…*that* much. However, I couldn't deny the fact that Marlene did live in 11A, the same apartment all the women from El Salvador lived in, as well. I also couldn't deny the fact that Trevor had said on multiple occasions there was a disturbance there.

"Do you think the woman who screamed in Apartment 14B was a ghost?" I asked.

"I don't know."

"What did she look like?" I asked.

"She had on black pants, white tennis shoes, and she had a big straw hat on. I didn't see her face, but she walked with a limp."

"Can ghosts limp?" I asked.

Marlene had no idea, so we Googled it.

Google didn't know either.

Shoot.

Chase returned and pulled me aside. "The apartment was unlocked, and the attic door was open."

Great. "I'm not a hundred percent positive if I locked the front door. I did close the attic." It was an awkward door to open and close, and I remembered making sure it was sealed tight before I left. "Marlene said her apartment is haunted by a woman. The ghost was young with dark hair."

Chase blinked. "What does that have to do with anything?"

"Read your text messages. There was a group of women from El Salvador who lived in Apartment 11A around the time the victim was killed. They ranged in ages from twenty to late thirties. None of them have move-out inspections, and some lived here when Alvin and Sherman did. By the way, I sent you their last names, social security numbers, and birthdates. Sherman is the one who has a criminal record."

"Interesting. I'll look at the information right now."

"What about this woman who ran screaming from Apartment 14B?"

"Someone was clearly in the attic. I'm going to request patrol to come around here in case she returns."

"You don't think my residents are in danger, do you?"

"Not unless one of your residents is a killer." The goats screamed again, and Chase cocked his thumb to Fox's apartment. "That guy might be in danger. I'd kill him if he were my neighbor."

"Don't even joke about it. I'm maxed out on homicides," I said, rubbing my chest.

Note to self: Buy Tums before you go home.

"Have you talked to Patrick?" Chase asked.

Ugh. Right. That. I'd almost forgotten. "Yes, he's getting out of property management all together."

"I'm not buying it," Chase said. "He's dodging us."

"He said you were playing phone tag."

"Phone tag insinuates that he has called us back."

"That doesn't make sense. It's *Patrick.*"

"You need to accept the possibility that your boss may have been involved."

"But he's married and has kids and dogs."

"Do you know how many men I've put away who are married with kids and dogs at home?" he asked.

I shook my head. Patrick wasn't a killer. Sure, I'd entertained the thought, but only for a moment. I *knew* him. There's no way. Not buying it. "The person running from Apartment 14B was a woman, though. Patrick is a man."

"He has a wife, right?"

"*Yes.*"

Note to self: Check if Patrick's wife has a limp.

"I need to finish talking to Marlene. Before I go, I'd really appreciate it if you went to dinner on Friday with me. Hampton is my partner, and that is a very important relationship."

There weren't enough words in the English language to express how deeply I did not want to go out to dinner with Silvia Kravitz. But I loved Chase, and he loved his partner, and his partner loved Silvia. What else could I say but, "Are you sure we have to go?"

"Yes."

"Fine," I said with a sigh.

"Thank you, Cambria." His words were laced with relief, and he gave me a quick kiss. "I'll make it up to you tonight."

Oh, boy.

CHAPTER THIRTEEN

———

Exceptional researching skills

I stopped at Costco for a four-pack of Tums, grabbed a smoothie from the food court, and went home. No new messages waited for me in the office, and I sat behind my desk and wiggled the mouse to wake up the computer. My mind went back to what Marlene had said about the ghost in her apartment. I felt a little ridiculous for even entertaining the idea…but what if? Who's to say what happens after we die? Maybe the woman in the barrel was stuck in a purgatory, waiting for someone to come along and discover her body?

I decided to Google purgatory and, *wowza*, there was a lot of information on the internet regarding the intermediate state between life and death. After an hour of research, I was pretty confident Los Angeles was one giant purgatory. Luckily, my phone rang and saved me from the rabbit hole I'd found myself in.

A number I didn't recognize flashed across the screen, and I answered. "Hello."

"Cambria Clyne, this is Alvin Leo," said the caller. "I received your message on Facebook. You found something of mine in the attic?"

OK, I may have been vague in my message to Alvin, asking him to please call me regarding the personal effects I'd found in the attic. Not really a lie, more so a…fine, that was a lie, and I felt bad. But I had a hunch he wouldn't have called me back if I'd told him why I was calling.

"Yes, thank you for calling me back. I appreciate it. We did find a something that I think could have belonged to you. Since I have you on the phone, I was hoping you could give me information about your former roommate."

"What did he do now?" he said with groan.

"Did he have a relationship with any of the women who lived in Apartment 11A?"

"Sure, he dated Larissa for a few months."

Aha! I silently celebrated with a fist pump. I was close. I could feel it. With Alvin on speaker, I pulled up the name and pictures of the women from Apartment 11A, except there wasn't a Larissa on file. "Are you sure she lived in Apartment 11A?"

"I'm pretty sure. It's been at least forty-something years."

Then the timing wouldn't work. The name Larissa did sound familiar, though.

"What items of mine did you find?" Alvin asked.

Oh. Right. That. Shoot. "I found…a-a pillow."

"A pillow?"

"Yes, a pillow. I heard you had a friend who slept up in the attic a few times. Maybe it's his? Do you have his name and number?"

"We didn't have a friend sleep up there. That was Sherman. He'd run into financial trouble and sublet his room, and he decided to sleep in the attic before management found out."

I wrote this down on a pad of paper. If Sherman slept in the attic, then he had plenty of time to hide the barrel up there.

"About the pillow," Alvin said. "You can go ahead and toss it."

"Are you sure?"

"Positive."

Good, because the medical examiner had confiscated the pillow anyway. I would have gone to buy him a new one if he'd really wanted it.

"Also…um…about the black bags," I said. "I heard you had quite a few up there as well."

"What about them?"

"What was inside?"

"Props. Wood. Stuff for the set. We worked on a show over at the lot."

I figured "the lot" meant Warner Bros. Made sense, and I had serious doubt he'd tell me if there was a body in any of them. But it couldn't hurt to ask. "There didn't happened to be a dead body in any of those black bags?"

So Alvin hung up on me, and I immediately called Chase.

"How exactly did you get this information about Sherman Varner?" he asked.

"Kevin and I looked through the archives." I picked up a paperclip and began unwinding it.

"I've got a detective from Lompoc going to see him today. And these women are the ones from El Salvador who you told me about?"

"Yes."

"I went ahead and ran all the names. The three women who stood out to me are Gabriela Lopez—she moved in September of 1991, but there is no record of her after. Same with Lupita Gomez. She moved in on September 5, 1994, and there is no record of her either. Maria Lopez left the country in 1979, moved back to El Salvador, and then she moved back to the States in 1993 and listed the Burbank building Apartment 11A as her address, but there is no record of her after."

"Did you happen to find any information on a woman named Larissa?"

"You didn't send me her info."

"Sherman dated her in the seventies."

"The body hasn't been there that long," Chase said.

That's right. But, *dang*, the name Larissa sounded familiar.

CHAPTER FOURTEEN

Proficient in the art of self-defense

Even though I had called in sick, I went ahead and worked until six o'clock. Tom had Lilly for the night, and I had Amy and Kevin curled up on my couch. Kevin with the first Zankla book and Amy with the second. I could have pranced around in a pony costume and they wouldn't have noticed. They were completely lost in the world of Borbank.

"Reena's book signing is in an hour. Would anyone like dinner?" I asked from the kitchen, pulling out leftover pizza.

"Mmmhmmm," both Amy and Kevin said.

"I'm making split pea soup with a side of peanuts. Sound good?"

"Mmmhmmm."

They were obviously not paying attention. Kevin hated peas, and Amy was allergic to nuts. Whatever. I wasn't going to waste my cold pizza on those who wouldn't fully appreciate it. Not that Amy consumed carbs anyway.

I sat at my kitchen table and ate in silence. Every few minutes Amy or Kevin would gasp or laugh. At one point, Amy had tears slithering down the side of her cheeks, carving grooves in her makeup. I felt like an outsider, sitting there with my pizza, watching them read.

I finished my dinner, rinsed my plate, and changed my clothes. "We're leaving in twenty minutes," I said.

"Mmmhmmm."

"You two get ready. I'll be right back."

"Mmmmhmmm."

I walked to the third courtyard and up to Mr. and Mr. Nguyen's apartment. I could hear the faint hum of the television. At one point, they were both hard of hearing, and they'd have the

TV up to max volume. After Mr. Nguyen landed the job, Patrick paid for hearing aids for them both. A beautiful gesture from a man with a good, *non*-murderous heart.

Mrs. Nguyen answered and frowned. "You're too pale. Come in."

I stepped into her apartment, and she locked the door behind me. They had a one-bedroom unit. In my opinion, the one-bedrooms were the best floor plan in the community. Big kitchen, spacious living room, hall bathroom, and a bedroom with two walk-in closets. They were easy to rent, and I'd miss showing them.

"Is Mr. Nguyen here?" I asked.

"No, he went to Home Depot to pick up a part for something. That man never stops working. I tell him to come home at five, but he won't step foot through that door until everything is done. Why? What's wrong?"

I fidgeted with my fingers. "Patrick is quitting."

"How can he quit if he owns the business?"

"He's closing."

For a moment, Mrs. Nguyen was silent. "What does this mean for us?" she finally asked.

"It means a new management company will take over, and they'll likely bring their own staff with them."

Mrs. Nguyen sat on the table and folded her hands.

"But there's still a chance that Mr. Nguyen will stay," I quickly added and slid into the seat beside her. "He's so good at what he does. Anyone would be lucky to have him."

"No one will hire a man of his age. They want young things."

"No, that's not true." OK, that was true. It would be harder to get a maintenance job as a sixty-something. Crud. I felt even worse.

"I was worried about this," she said. "Last time I talked to Patrick, he sounded too tired. I told him he should eat more meat, but he didn't listen to me." I loved how she felt upping your protein intake would solve any problem.

"I'm so sorry."

"What do you have to say sorry for?"

"It's my fault. He heard I'd interviewed next door, and it seems to be the straw that broke the camel's back."

Mrs. Nguyen squeezed my arm. "If that made him quit, then we don't want to work for him anyway. You deserve to move up in your career."

But they didn't deserve to lose theirs. "What will you do?"

"My sister has been begging us to move to New Mexico to be closer to her. It might be time to leave California. This state is getting crazy anyway. I'm tired of being charged for every little thing."

I felt light-headed with panic. "You can't leave!"

"We're getting old, and it's too expensive around here. Do you know I paid five dollars a gallon to fill up my car yesterday? Robbery."

"B-b-b-but…" I couldn't think of a rebuttal. She was right. Los Angeles was expensive. If my job hadn't included housing, I have no idea how I would have put food on the table. But… "You can't leave!"

"Nothing is set in stone. Calm down. You are making me anxious."

I couldn't calm down. Not now. If I'd known I'd lose the Nguyens, I would have torn up Dr. Dashwood's card and never given the job a second thought. "What about Lilly?" Perhaps I could guilt her into changing her mind. "She'll miss you too much."

"We think of Lilly as our grandchild. It would be hard, but don't get ahead of yourself. We need to lose the job first."

"Right." I wiped a tear because of course I was crying. How could I do life without the Nguyens close by? They were my neighbors when I had Lilly. Mrs. Nguyen taught me how to parent. They were family. I could not lose them.

I would *not* lose them.

"No," I said, feeling a surge of determination. "This is not going to happen. I will fix this." I marched to the door.

"What are you going to do?" Mrs. Nguyen asked.

"I have a plan."

OK, not so much a plan, but I had an idea.

Well, more so a long shot.

First, I had to make sure this woman in the barrel story didn't get out to the press. Otherwise my plan would not work.

* * *

When I got back to my apartment, Kevin and Amy were in the exact spots I'd left them. "We need to leave," I said, and stormed to my office.

Amy blinked a few times. "Where are we going?"

"To the Reena Hike book signing. It's tonight. Remember?"

"Oh, good." Amy reached over and yanked her book from Kevin's hands.

"Hey, I was reading that."

"I want Reena to sign these," she said.

"We're meeting Reena?" Kevin asked.

"Honestly, you two don't listen to a word I say." I flung open my office door and grabbed my phone, which I'd left on my desk. A scrap of paper near my calculator caught my attention.

Francis Holland, Tammy Whitewood, and Larissa Lopez.

I dropped to my chair, the paper clutched in my hand. *Larissa.* These were the women from the missing person website. I knew Larissa sounded familiar. Just as I was sure there were a lot of women named Larissa.

I pulled up the missing person website once again and scrolled down until I found her. Larissa *Lopez.* The same last name as so many of the roommates who had lived in Apartment 11A. She fit the description of the woman in the barrel perfectly. Petite. Only five foot two. She had a thin and vibrant face with dark hair and dark eyes. Larissa was only twenty years old and last seen on October 23, 1978, in Los Angeles, California.

She certainly matched the description of the woman in the barrel, except for the fact that she had almost all her teeth. But the timing didn't work at all. Although...I crunched the numbers on my calculator. Larissa would have been in her midthirties in 1996, when only four barrels were moved.

I went to Google and searched *Larissa Lopez disappearance* and landed on a page called The Charley Project.

A website that profiled over 13,000 cold missing person cases. Larissa's profile gave the same information as the government page did.

Date missing: October 23, 1978

Missing from: Los Angeles

Classification: missing

Date of birth: August 20, 1958

Age: 20 years old

Height and weight: 5'2, 101 pounds

Distinguishing characteristics: has a brown front tooth and is missing both canine teeth.

Details of disappearance: Lopez was last seen at a Charlotte Russe department store in Los Angeles, California on October 23, 1978. She has not been heard from since. Few details are available on this case.

Shoot.

* * *

We drove to Hollywood. My mind churned over the information I'd discovered about Larissa. There were a lot of holes in that theory. She was too young when she went missing, and she had most of her teeth. Could she have been kidnapped? Held hostage for eighteen years until she was finally killed? What kidnapper would pay for teeth implants for a fixed denture? This could be a farfetched idea, or this could be a possibility. I'd sent a text to Chase, asking him to call me as soon as the detectives finished with Sherman. If he was already in prison, he might have confessed to other crimes.

Right?

Hollywood and Highland was exceptionally busy, and I ended up having to pay twenty dollars to park five blocks away. The line to meet Reena was already down the street and around the corner. Luckily, we had our front-of-the-line pass, which I flashed to the security guard at the door. We were escorted to the back of the store, where Reena Hike sat behind a table with her books proudly displayed. She was older than her picture on the internet, but she had the same purple streaked hair and wore a tight pleather jumpsuit.

"Welcome to the Horror Eclipse." Reena had a husky voice. "Thank you for coming."

Amy shoved me out of the way, and I nearly tumbled into a shelf carrying fake machetes.

At least, I think they were fake.

"You have no idea what your books mean to me." Amy was on the verge of tears. "I personally relate to Zankla's best friend, Meola. I'm an actress. You might have seen me on *Ghost Confidential* or *Celebrity Tango*." She placed her stack of books in front of Reena. "I'm a huge fan."

"Congratulations," Reena said, not bothering to look up, and began signing the inside of Amy's paperbacks. I took the opportunity to step in.

"My name is Cambria Clyne, and I'm the apartment manager for the Burbank building you used to manage."

Reena froze with the pen in her hand and gazed up. "Cambria *Clyne*?"

"*Yes*. And this is Kevin McMills." I cocked a thumb towards Kevin and did a double take. He had a purple dot on his forehead. Not sure where that came from or what exactly it meant.

"I'm with the werewolves," he said, as if this explained everything.

Anyway. "He's also a fan of the series," I said to Reena. "I'd like to talk to you about your time as a manager. Not now, of course. But if you have time afterward or if we could chat on the phone…" my voice trailed off. Mostly because Reena's face had blanched.

Amy put her mouth up to my ear. "Don't tick her off, please. I need this part."

I wasn't trying to, but I suspected she knew something.

After a pause, Reena snapped the book closed, looking more composed. "We're having a launch party in the back as soon as I'm done. Meet me there."

"Sure." That was easy.

Almost too easy.

I thanked her profusely, and we were escorted through beaded curtains. The room was dim, the walls were dark, and the black lights hurt my eyes. Pictures of the main characters were displayed on easels, and there was a sandwich station filled with delicious-looking meats.

Don't mind if I do.

I checked my phone to see if Chase had texted me back. Nope. All I had was an email from Silvia Kravitz—once again—confirming our dinner reservations for Friday at six o'clock. *Ugh.*

"This place is awesome." Amy had a pink cocktail in her hand and a purple dot on her forehead.

Note to self: Read the books.

I felt left out.

"Imagine what the movie premiere will look like," she said.

Kevin walked up behind her, cracking open a Coke. "This place is like an acid trip." He took a sip of his soda then spewed it all over my face.

"Kevin!" I was drenched. Gross.

Amy put a hand over her drink. "What did you do that for?"

I grabbed a napkin from the table and followed Kevin's gaze. "Oh, my gosh."

On an easel was a picture of a frowny old man with a purple face and red teardrops sliding down his cheeks. Underneath was the name of the character: *Enest McMall.*

"I've never heard of him before," Amy said. "He must not appear until book twelve."

I swiped a book displayed on a table and read the back.

Tarian people...werewolves...yada, yada, yada...up against the greedy landlord, Enest McMall.

Wow. Subtle. Real subtle.

"What do you make of this?" I asked Kevin.

It was hard to tell in the dark lighting, but he appeared to be crying.

"Oh, Kevin." Amy gave him a hug, careful not to spill her drink. "Don't be sad."

Suddenly, he burst into an all-consuming, noiseless laughter.

"What is so funny?" I asked.

"The...the...the..." He sucked in a breath. "That's freaking hilarious. My dad is in the book."

"You don't know it's your dad," Amy said.

"His name is Ernest McMills," I said.

"Well then, yeah, it's your dad." She took a sip of her drink.

I put the book down when I heard a "*Psst*" and looked around. It was Reena, hidden behind one of the easels, gesturing for me to follow her.

"But what about—" I started to say, but Reena had already walked away. It was hard to see in the dark room, but the purple streaks in her hair glowed under the black lights, and I followed her out the back door.

We stepped into an alleyway. Reena rushed me and shoved me backwards. I lost my footing and fell into a pile of trash bags.

"What are you—"

She slapped a hand over my mouth. I smacked her arm away and rolled off the pile.

"You're not going anywhere." Reena grabbed my belt loop and pulled me back. "I refuse to be bullied."

Bullied? She must not understand what the definition of a bully is. Holy hell, this woman was nuts! If this was what years of property management did to a person, I quit.

"You're the one who attacked me!" I elbowed her in the ribs, and she stumbled into the wall, holding her side. We were both out of breath and staring at each other, calculating our next move. I checked over my shoulder. The alleyway had a dead end. I'd have to go past Reena to get out of there. So I made a run for it.

She was surprisingly fast for a woman wearing pleather. "You can tell the McMillses that I will write whatever I want!" She had me in a headlock.

I stomped on her foot, and she loosened her grip. "I'm…not telling the…McMillses anything," I choked out. "I work for a property management company."

"You don't get to dictate what I write."

"You're…being…ridiculous," I rasped, still in a chokehold, and I bit her arm. What can I say? I fight scrappy.

Reena let me go, and I fell to my hands and knees and crawled behind the dumpster for cover.

"You have some nerve," she said. "I cannot believe you brought a McMills to my launch party. Neo was wrong about you!"

"I have no idea what you're talking about. Kevin is estranged from his parents. He hasn't spoken to them since they kicked him out when he was eighteen. He hates them just as much as you apparently do."

Silence fell, and I dared to look around the dumpster. Reena was out of breath. Her forehead glistened, and she had a pipe in her hand. Yikes.

"He's Dolores and Ernest's child?" Her voice had less of an edge to it. "I thought he was the trustee."

"No, you're thinking of Trevor McMills. He's the lawyer over the trust."

Reena dropped the pipe. I staggered to my feet, keeping my arms up, ready to attack. This woman was wacko.

"Sorry for being a little aggressive," she said.

A little aggressive? That was like saying the sun was a little hot.

She drew in a breath, unzipped her jumpsuit slightly, and fanned her face. "You have to understand where I am coming from. I get a letter from the McMills's attorney at least once a month, threatening to ruin me if I don't stop writing."

"From Trevor?" It was hard to imagine Trevor threatening *anyone*.

"They can't touch me, though," Reena said. "I created a world, and sure, I drew from my own experiences, but who is to say it's the McMills I'm writing about?"

"Your villain is named *Enest McMall*."

"Pfft." She waved, dismissing my statement. "It could be anyone."

Sure.

"Put your hands down," she said, as if I were being ridiculous. "I'm not going to touch you. My old maintenance guy, Neo, told me you'd be coming by. He also told me about the woman in the barrel found in the attic. You think Sherman or Alvin from Apartment 2B had something to do with it?"

I eyed the closest exit points. "When did he tell you?"

"Yesterday. He called while I was here doing a book signing. Said it was urgent."

"Is that why you left early?"

She nodded. "I had to check on something."

"Did you go to the Burbank building?"

"No, I hate that place."

"Then what did you need to check on?"

Reena sized me up, as if deciding if she could trust me. "Manager to manager?"

That was code for "between you and me." At least, I thought it was. No one had actually said "manager to manager" to me before. Anyway. "Sure."

"I had to check with my lawyer before I talked to the cops," she said. "I don't need nothing jeopardizing my livelihood."

"Are you saying that… What exactly are you saying?"

"Working at the Burbank building was a stressful situation. I'm able to talk about my experiences now openly without using names. It's been therapeutic."

Ah. Got it. "So you don't want to talk to the police because you don't want to risk fans finding out how close to the truth your books are?"

"Bingo."

"Do you know anything about this woman?"

She let out a short laugh. "Let me tell you something about Ernest McMills. That man was the biggest cheapskate I'd ever met. When we had a vacancy, he'd give me a forty-dollar budget to turn the unit. Forty bucks! Then he'd get upset when it didn't rent right away."

I wasn't following. "So you think he killed the woman in the barrel?"

"Nah, he wasn't the violent type. He was just annoying. My point is, the man hated parting with his money. Then one day, out of the blue, he announced that they'd formed a trust and were grooming his nephew to take over. And between you and me, that kid was an idiot. Total meathead jock-type. I know he played football, and I think he took too many hits to the head. I have no idea how he graduated high school, let alone college. It made no sense for Dolores and Ernest to pass their fortune down to him."

"I think they were having problems with their son," I said, unsure of why I suddenly felt the need to defend the McMillses. Could be because she called Trevor a meathead when I rather liked him. Not that I'd say that in front of Reena. She'd probably stab me.

"I heard that, too. Sad story, actually. But back to Sherman and Alvin. We ended up giving them a thirty-day notice right before Elder Management took over. Their apartment was the last one I had to turn there."

This was a lot of information to mull over. The timing of everything, from Trevor taking over, Sherman and Alvin getting kicked out, Kevin being disowned, and Patrick entering the picture. I knew they happened around the same time. But it appeared they all happened *at* the same time.

"What about Dolores?" I asked. "His wife."

"Mrs. McMills didn't come around much. When she did, I hid. She talked down to Neo and me like we were the help. The Dolorad Witch of the Tarian Clan is based on her. The real Dolores complained about *everything*. Captain Tightwad was easier to deal with."

I assumed Captain Tightwad was Ernest. It was hard to keep up with the real names, fictional names, and nicknames. "Do you think Sherman or Alvin killed this woman in the barrel?"

"Sherman was a loose cannon. Horrible temper. If there were a problem, I'd wait for Alvin to get home. Once, Sherman broke a step with one of those damn black bags filled with set props that they'd drag to and from their apartment. I handed him an invoice, saying he'd need to pay for the repair. It was like he was possessed. His eyes went black, and he cursed me out. I told Ernest about the encounter, and he brushed it off. He didn't care. The day Sherman left was one of happiest days of my time as a property manager. Then, about a week later, a woman came around asking for him. This was right before I was fired."

I wanted to ask why she was fired, but then I remembered what Neo said. Elder Property Management took over, and he let everyone go. Also, I didn't want to ruin her concentration.

"I was inspecting Apartment 2B," she continued, "when the woman showed up. She was dressed real cute. Had on black flowy pants with white feathers printed near the bottom, and a sheer white shirt. I remember asking her where she got her clothes. Then I went and bought myself a pair of those pants, and they set me back almost sixty bucks. Anyway. She wanted to know where Sherman was. I told her that he'd moved out and I couldn't legally give her his forwarding address, and she left. She said they were friends back in the day, and she had come into town and needed his help. I asked what kind of help, assuming it had something to do with the movie business. She wouldn't say. Then two days later, I was there cleaning out my office when I heard two people arguing. It was the new property manager…what was his name?"

A lump formed in my throat. "Do you mean Patrick?"

"That's right. Patrick Elder. He and the woman were having a heated discussion. I totally eavesdropped because…well, why not? The fight was over a child. She wanted to see her kid, and he told her that was impossible. She kept pressing and pressing and crying and crying. I remember he was empathetic, but kept saying it was impossible."

"Child?" I squeaked out. "Where was the child?"

"I don't know. It struck me as odd, because she was looking for Sherman then was in a fight with Patrick, talking about a kid. And she was wearing the same outfit."

"Where did she say her clothes came from?"

Reena had to think. "Charlotte Russe."

I gulped. "Did you catch her name?"

"I don't remember. Maybe Lara? That sounds slightly familiar."

Lara *was* close to Larissa. It was possible that I was trying to fit a square peg into a round hole and Larissa had nothing to do with this. But still, even if there were so many similarities, the timing didn't work.

"Was her name Larissa?"

"Can't remember."

"What about the woman's teeth?"

Reena crinkled her nose. "Her teeth?"

"Where her teeth nice?"

"Not sure. Who looks at people's teeth?"

Me. "Was the woman petite with dark hair and Hispanic?"

"Yes. She was all three. As soon as Neo told me about the woman in the barrel, I immediately remembered this story. It has to be her. What are the chances? I mean, she was in a fight with Patrick the day Neo and I left for good. So I can't say what happened afterward. But I know for a fact there were five barrels in that attic. The resident in Apartment 4B would complain all the time about them. She thought they'd come crashing down on her head if there was an earthquake. Then she'd complain if Neo had to go in her apartment to use the attic access. We stored all the odds and ends for the property in those barrels."

On a whim, I grabbed my phone and pulled up the missing person website to the picture of Larissa. "Was this the woman?"

Reena grabbed my phone and zoomed in on the picture. "The woman I saw was older. Late thirties, maybe early forties. This could have been her when she was young. I can't say for sure." Not exactly helpful, but even if the woman wasn't Larissa, it sounded like whoever was arguing with Patrick could have been who ended up in the barrel.

I thanked Reena for her time. She apologized again for attacking me, and I left. My head felt heavy with all the new information. The woman in the Charlotte Russe outfit arguing with Patrick over a child. Not a baby, but a *child*. Could it have been Patrick's ex-wife? Did Patrick even have an ex-wife? I knew Patrick had a current wife. I'd never met her, but Patrick and I were Facebook friends, and I'd seen her picture. She was tall and blonde with blue eyes and freckles. But how did this woman know Sherman *and* Patrick? There had to be some connection between the two men.

CHAPTER FIFTEEN

――――――

Designated driver

I met up with Kevin and Amy at the party. They were talking to a man with dark, shiny hair and a red scarf. The crowd had tripled since I'd stepped out, and a DJ had arrived. The music thumped in time with my heartbeat, and the room was about fifteen degrees hotter than when I left. Hazy chatter could be heard over the loud bass, and I caught a few bits of conversation as I snaked my way towards Kevin and Amy. People were wondering where Reena had gone.

Amy waved as I approached. "Wheres haves you been?!"

Wheres? Haves? How many of those pink drinks has she had?

"Five," Kevin said, as if reading my thoughts.

A waiter came by and took Amy's empty glass and gave her a new pink drink. I swiped it from his hand and took a sip. *Wowza.* There was enough alcohol packed in that tiny pink cocktail to get a small army drunk.

"Heys, that's my…drink." Amy pouted.

"I think we're done."

"No. I don't want to be done. You have to meet…what's your name?" she asked the scarf guy.

Scarf guy stood a little taller. "Nathan."

"Yes, that's right. This is Zack. He is a producer and wants to get me a parts in the movies."

"Errr…um, I'm a book blogger." Nathan handed me a business card. "I blog about books."

Kevin laughed.

"This isn't funny," I hissed. "Let's get you out of here." I snaked an arm around Amy's tiny waist and escorted her through the crowd.

"Where did you go?" Kevin asked as we zigzagged around waiters and tables and people with purple faces on our way to the flashing EXIT sign.

"I had a run-in with Reena. She had *a lot* to say."

"Like what?"

"I'll tell you later. We need to get Amy home."

"Why? I'm finnntthh!" she slurred. "I want to sstay—"
She stopped to puke all over my shoes.

Gross.

* * *

We made it back to my apartment, only having to pull over twice so Amy could disgorge the contents of her stomach. What a night. I'd been puked on, spit on, and attacked by a woman in pleather. I was tired and ready for bed, but first I had a few pressing issues to deal with. One of which was my boyfriend, who was exiting his car just as we pulled up.

I'd completely forgotten Chase was coming over tonight.

"What happened to Amy?" Chase asked.

"Too many Tarian cocktails," Kevin said.

Chase looked to me for clarification.

"We were at Reena Hike's launch party." I managed to coax Amy out of the car. "She's been so busy reading today that she forgot to eat. Then she had too many drinks."

Amy started to protest, then paused to burp into her fist. "Yeah, maybe I did."

Chase took over escorting duties and grabbed Amy by the arm and slung it over his shoulders. I rolled my neck, from side to side working out a kink. I'd hauled a drunk Amy around many times over the course of our friendship—you'd think my body would be used to it by now.

"I'm going home," Kevin announced. "I want to finish this." He held up the latest Zankla book.

"I thought you were only on the first one?"

"I'm skipping ahead. I need to read about Enest McMall." He unleashed a devious grin, and I could see the muscles tense up a little in his jaw. I imagined these past few days had to have brought up a lot of painful memories. I wanted to ask him how he was feeling. But I knew if I brought up the subject, he'd make some sort of snarky remark and walk away.

But I couldn't help myself.

"Kevin, how are *you* doing?" I touched his arm.

"I'm feeling nauseated because you stink. Take a shower and call me in the morning."

At least he was predictable.

Back in my apartment, I found Amy passed out on the couch with a pillow under her head and a blanket pulled up to her chin. Chase was in the kitchen pouring a glass of water. He had on a gray suit. His tie was pulled loose and his hair disheveled. His five o'clock shadow was more a beard by this point, and his eyes were tired.

He was thrashed, and my heart swelled. It felt good having him in my home, and I couldn't help myself. I grabbed his stubbly cheeks and kissed him softly on the lips.

"What was that for?" he asked, running his fingers down the length of my spine.

"I missed you. That's all."

"Oh, yeah?" He gave me a mischievous smile. "How much?"

I playfully held my finger and thumb about an inch apart, and Chase hoisted me up onto the counter. I wrapped my legs around him, and his mouth traveled down my neck, leaving a trail of passionate kisses. I threw my head back and allowed all my worries to float away…for a moment.

Like a freaking boomerang, they all came shooting back at me with a vengeance.

A flashback to four months ago played out in my mind. I was perched on the bathroom counter, my legs wrapped around Tom, who was kissing my neck. It had been the first time Tom and I had kissed since the night we made Lilly. His lips were warm and wanting, and I was swept up in a moment of passion. If we hadn't been interrupted by a grumpy three-year-old who wanted breakfast, then who knows what would have happened.

I was so lost in thought that I hadn't noticed that Chase was still kissing me along my jawline.

Right. Be in the moment, Cambria.

I sucked in a deep breath and lowered my mouth to meet his. We kissed with more fervor and passion, but my mind continued to wander off.

What if I accepted Tom's proposal?

We'd get married. Move in together. Tom had mentioned leaving the state. Of course, I'd have to bring Mr. and Mrs. Nguyen along. Sure, they had family in New Mexico, but I called dibs. Tom would go work for a law firm, and I'd find a job in property management there. We'd have more kids.

It was a happy thought. Until I realized if I went with Tom, I'd no longer have Chase. I had serious doubts Tom would be cool with me bringing along my ex-boyfriend. There was also Kevin. I couldn't leave him either. Nor could I ditch Amy.

Really, everyone would have to come along.

On the other hand, what if I married Chase?

We'd stay here in Los Angeles. He'd move in. I'd keep my job—assuming I had one. He'd go off to train for the FBI then come back and work. We could do this until his new job relocated us someplace new. I couldn't up and leave without Tom's consent. He'd have to agree to come along—which he wouldn't. Not easily, at least. I could still bring the Nguyens, and Kevin, and Amy.

Really, the only way I could have both men in my life was to accept Chase.

Or I could accept no one.

That was also a real option. Especially since Lilly had decided she no longer liked having Chase around. I had no idea what that was about. What I knew for certain was that I could never be with a man my child didn't like.

"What's wrong?" Chase asked, his voice husky. He cupped my face in his hands, studying me with his gorgeous green eyes.

Right, making out. Focus, Cambria.

I forced my mouth to make words. "We should talk."

"I know."

"Can you either talk louder so I can hear or go to your room?!" Amy shouted from the couch. "I haven't fully passed out yet."

I rolled my eyes and leapt off the counter. Chase grabbed my hand and pulled me down the hall. With each step, my feet started to protest. They wanted to go back to the kitchen and make out, not deal with the gigantic elephant in the room. Both figuratively and literally, as Lilly's stuffed elephant Amy had bought her was on the floor next to my bed.

"Where did that come from?" Chase asked.

"A present from Aunt Amy."

"Why is it cross-eyed?"

"Not sure."

"How much did that thing cost?"

"Fifty dollars."

"It's creepy." Chase moved the gigantic stuff animal back to the closet and loosened his tie with a yawn.

"Rough day?" I asked.

"You have no idea."

"How'd it go at the prison with Sherman?"

Chase crossed the room and fell onto the bed face first. "Sherman doesn't know where Larissa is," he muffled into the pillow then turned his head. "I pulled the case file. Larissa was originally from El Salvador, except she had dual citizenship. Her mother was a US citizen, and Larissa was born here. Then they moved to Central America where her father was from. When she was eighteen, she came back and lived with her aunt in Los Angeles. Her aunt is the one who reported her missing. I spoke to her today, and I'm just not so sure this is our girl."

Shoot. It was a long shot anyway. "What did the aunt say?"

Chase rolled to his side and propped up on his elbow. "This is between you and me. Got it?"

I gave him a captain salute.

"Larissa did date Sherman," he said.

"Aha!"

"Hold the celebrating. There's more. Larissa dated Sherman for six months. They'd originally met at the apartment complex. Larissa was *friends* with a few of the women who did live there in Apartment 11A. She never lived there."

Still, I mentally patted myself on the back.

"Everything lines up but the timing," he says. "Larissa has the right body type. She was Hispanic. She had connections to the Burbank building. Her aunt even said she was self-conscious about her smile and had been saving up to have dental work done. Larissa had been going out a lot with a mystery man. When her aunt questioned who it was, Larissa refused to answer. It wasn't Sherman. He was interviewed back in '78, and the detective wrote that he was cleared as a suspect. They even searched his apartment, and nothing turned up. The detective who interviewed him today said Sherman was adamant that he did not hurt Larissa. According to him, the two were friends after they broke up, and she'd been acting aloof right before she vanished. I checked with the medical examiner, and he's confident that the body has not been dead over forty years. It can't be her unless she vanished, reappeared twenty years later, and was then killed."

"Well, now that you mention it. I had an interesting conversation with Reena Hike tonight." I rubbed my neck at the memory, then launched into what Reena had told me about the woman who showed up at Sherman's apartment. I left out the bit about Reena basing the story line of her hit books on her time at Burbank—not that it wasn't already obvious. I mean, come on, *Bor*bank. But she said *manager to manager*, and I wasn't about to break code. Nor did I tell Chase about her attacking me. I didn't want to get her in trouble.

"She said her name was Lara?" Chase asked.

"Reena was shaky on some of the details, being that it was so long ago. She did say that the woman was first looking for Sherman then was fighting with Patrick over a kid."

"It would sure be nice if your boss wasn't hiding from us. His lawyer called us and said his client would only talk if he were present."

Oh, geez. Patrick was getting harder and harder to defend.

"Hampton also tried to get Reena to come down to the station today, but she refused. Said she'd only talk with her lawyer present, and her lawyer was out of town. Sounded to me like she had something to hide."

"Perhaps, but it's not a dead body." *I don't think.*

My phone rang, and I slid it out from my back pocket. A 704 number flashed across my screen. Probably a solicitor. "Where is 704 area code?"

"North Carolina," Chase said, because he knows pretty much everything.

North Carolina! This was Maria's cousin, Angela, the one who knew about everyone who lived in Apartment 11A.

I slapped the phone to my ear. "Hello?"

"Hola. Es esta Cambria?"

"This is Cambria."

"Recibí tu mensaje."

"Sorry, I don't speak Spanish."

"Recibí tu mensaje," she repeated.

Crud. *Why can't I speak Spanish?*

"Give it to me," Chase said.

Oh, that's right. I handed over the phone, and he spoke in Spanish with such fluidity you'd think it was his first language.

Note to self: Learn a second language.

With Lilly able to speak in Vietnamese and Chase able to speak in like ten different languages, I felt a wee bit inadequate.

Chase looked at me, his brows squished together. "She says you left her a message about her cousin who is dead in a barrel?"

"That's not what I said." More or less. "She's related to all the women who lived in Apartment 11A, and her cousin Maria said she keeps tabs on everyone."

Chase first looked heavenward then put the phone back to his ear. He spoke for several minutes. My Spanish was limited, but I heard him mention a few of the women from my list.

"Everyone is alive," he said. "The women I didn't have information on have all moved back to El Salvador." Chase returned to the phone and asked about Larissa. "She said Larissa was her cousin Maria's cousin's friend on her other side."

That wasn't confusing. "Does she know anyone by the name of Lara?"

Chase asked. "Larissa sometimes went by Lara."

I threw my arms up in a silent victory, and Chase gave me a high five. This was too much of a coincidence to be a coincidence. The only thing that didn't work was the timing. There had to be an explanation as to why Larissa went missing for...I did the math on my calculator...exactly eighteen years.

Chase finally hung up and heaved a telling sigh.

Except I wasn't quite sure what it was telling me.

"What? What? What? What?" I asked. "What?"

"Again, it sounds like Larissa could be our girl. It's just the timing."

"Did Angela say anything about a child?"

"She suspected Larissa got involved with a married man and took off. She confirmed Larissa had been sneaking around with a guy she refused to identify, but again, the timing does not work."

I felt like yelling, *I know the timing—Does. Not. Work!* But I didn't. The walls were thin, and Mickey, my upstairs neighbor, was already asleep. He kept to a strict schedule. He'd be up in two hours to go to the bathroom. Anyway. "What if Larissa did take off and returned eighteen years later and was killed?"

Chase shrugged, as if to say *maybe*. "According to her aunt, Larissa wouldn't have taken off without contacting her parents."

"Have you talked to her parents? Maybe she did contact them."

Again with the shrug. "Her parents are dead. Mother died in '87 from cancer. Dad died in '85 from a heart attack."

"It's too much a coincidence that Reena said a woman by the name of Lara came by Sherman's empty apartment right before Reena was fired. The woman left and returned a few days later and got into a fight with Patrick about a child. If she had the child in '78, the kid would be eighteen in 1996." I checked the math on my phone. *Yep.* "The woman was wearing black pants and a white shirt that she'd bought at Charlotte Russe."

Chase froze. "Did the pants have white feathers?"

"Yes, near the bottom…what are you doing? Who are you calling?"

"Hampton. Our woman in the barrel had black pants with white feathers around the bottom." He slapped his phone to his ear.

CHAPTER SIXTEEN

———

Excellent at solving murders

Hampton was at my front door roughly five minutes later since he'd been at Silvia's. He'd left his hair at home, which was nice. He looked better bald. We were sitting around my kitchen table. Amy had shuffled to my bedroom to continue to sober up, dragging her blanket behind her.

Hampton's extended forehead glistened under the light from the fan above my kitchen table—being as it was hot in my apartment. *So* hot. Now that I knew Mr. McMills was so cheap, it made sense that most of my ideas for improvement had been immediately shut down. Updated air conditioners for the Los Angeles property being one of them.

"Larissa Lopez disappeared in 1978," Hampton said for the fifth time since he arrived. "The timing doesn't work."

"Reena said the woman, *Lara*, looked nice. Like she had money," I said.

"Who would give her money?"

"I don't know. The married man she was sneaking around with? What I do know is that Larissa Lopez knew Sherman in Apartment 2B. She did disappear in 1978. Then a woman matching Larissa's description shows up eighteen years later, dressed nice, looking for Sherman. Then argued with Patrick about a child. Now we have a dead woman in a barrel wearing the same outfit that this Lara woman was last seen in. I think Larissa is Lara, and I think someone must have paid her to disappear."

Chase was studying his hands while I gave Hampton all the information. "If she had money, why was she wearing the same outfit?"

An excellent question. One I didn't have an answer to. I had zero experience having money. "I don't know. You should ask Reena. Just be careful—make sure you don't mention the McMillses."

Chase looked at me. "Why?"

Uh. "She doesn't like them. That's all."

Hampton twisted his mouth and turned his attention to me. "You're saying that Larissa Lopez disappeared for almost twenty years, reappeared, and then was killed?"

I felt like saying *seriously man, have you not been listening to me the entire time?* Instead I said, "It's a strong possibility," because even if he did wear his pants high, and he was dating my nightmare of a resident, and I was being forced to go on a double date, he was still a put-his-life-on-the-line-to-protect-and-serve-every-day cop. He deserved respect.

"We need to speak to Maria tomorrow," Chase said.

"Why wait until tomorrow? I have her number." My phone was already out, the line ringing in my ear, when I realized it was almost ten thirty. A little late, but this was important.

"Hola?" Maria answered, her voice throaty, like she'd just been jolted awake. *Oops.*

"Hi, Maria. It's Cambria—"

Hampton snatched the phone from my grasp and left the room.

"Hey, what did he do that for?"

"Cambria, you have to remember this is an active investigation, and despite what you think, you are not a detective."

"Pffft. I should be."

"We don't know anything for sure. And please don't talk about this to anyone." He gave me a look of warning.

I pretended to zip my lips.

Hampton returned. "Maria confirmed Larissa, who also went by Lara, disappeared in 1978. She did suspect Larissa was pregnant right before she vanished."

A horrid thought crept into my mind. What if Patrick was the father? What if they had a child? What if she returned and he killed her? Oh, no. I gasped so loudly, Chase smacked my back, assuming I'd just choked on my ice cream. Because, of course, I had a gallon of mint chip out. This was stressful!

"No...no..." I huffed out. "I'm fine. It's just...you don't think..." I didn't want to utter the words, but I had to. "You don't think she was in a relationship with Patrick. Do you? And this was all an awful attempt to cover up an affair?"

Chase and Hampton shared a look. Hampton gave his head a slight nod. Chase returned the nod, and the two headed right for the door.

Guess that is a yes?

CHAPTER SEVENTEEN

Wingman

It was hard to sleep for multiple reasons. One being that Amy was in my bed, snoring. The other was the thought of Patrick down at the police station, being grilled by Chase and Hampton. Even if Patrick decided not to quit, and I kept my job, and this whole Cedar Creek business never happened. My boyfriend interrogating my boss would surely have put a damper on our professional relationship.

I only hoped they hadn't completely discounted Sherman. The man was in jail for assault. Clearly he was capable of heinous crimes. He could have done this. The child Lara was speaking of could have been his. Why Patrick would have been involved was beyond me. According to both Reena and Patrick, the two unruly roommates had been kicked out before he even started working there.

I couldn't figure out what the connection between the three was.

The ceiling creaked when my upstairs neighbor, Mickey, got out of bed for his midnight bathroom break. I heard his *thump, thump, thump* across his bedroom floor, the slam of the toilet seat, and the *whoosh* of the toilet flushing.

Gotta love multifamily living.

I threw the covers off and walked myself to the bathroom. Though I didn't have to *go*. Instead, I splashed my face with water a few times and stared at my reflection in the mirror. My blue eyes were cradled in bags, and my face was void of color. If I hadn't had a pulse, I'd have sworn *I* was dead.

After a few more splashes of water, I determined sleep was not an option. I grabbed my pillow and was about to go to the living room when I heard the faint vibrating sound of my phone on the nightstand. This late, it was either the emergency line or news of the woman in the barrel.

I scrambled to answer before the call went to voice mail. *Kevin?*

"Hello," I whispered, tip-toeing out of the room.

"I'm at your door," Kevin said. "Open up."

"Why are you at my door?"

"I'll tell you when you open it."

I put my eye up to the peephole. "What have I told you about wearing clothes when you walk around the property?" I angry whispered.

"Open the damn door."

Fine. Fine. "Fine." As soon as I turned off the alarm and unlocked the deadbolt, Kevin exploded into the room. Face red, fists clenched, mouth swearing. He had on a pair of red boxers with *Groom* printed across the butt.

"What's wrong?" I asked.

"My sperm donor. That's what."

"Huh?"

"My father. Dad. Pop. Parent. Padre. Papa. Forebearer. He's a hypocrite." Kevin punched my table.

"Please don't take out your frustration on my furniture," I said.

"I want to hit something," he said through gritted teeth. "Rip something to shreds."

"Hold on." I ran back to my room and grabbed the elephant. "Go for it."

Kevin yanked the plush toy from my grasp and ripped its head off. It snowed stuffing as he continued to dismember the animal limb by limb, muttering profanity under his breath.

I decided to wait until he finished before I asked what had happened.

It took a while.

…still waiting…

I scooped us each a bowl of ice cream for when he finished.

…still waiting…

I polished off my bowl.

…still waiting…

I went ahead and ate Kevin's bowl, my eyes wide as I watched him shred the last bit of the stuffed animal.

He turned to face me, his chest rising and falling with rapid breaths. "Thanks."

"No problem."

"That felt good."

"I'm glad."

He looked around the room, taking in the mess he'd just made. "The kid's not going to cry over this, right?"

"No. She didn't like that thing anyway."

"Good. Because I didn't want to hear her get all whiney and you get all crazy."

I rolled my eyes. "Care to share why you showed up at my door in the middle of the night to mutilate my child's toy?"

"My dad is a hypocrite!"

"Caught that. How?"

Kevin marched to the kitchen and grabbed the box of generic Cheerios then searched the cabinet for a bowl. "When I told my parents I was gay, they freaked out. Told me it was immoral and all this crap. Then they sent me to a therapist who tried to treat me." He returned to the table with a mixing bowl filled to the brim with cereal. "When that didn't work, they exiled me here, and I haven't heard from them since. *Immoral*, Cambria."

"So you had all this pent-up anger, and now you're finally releasing it?" I asked, trying to understand why the sudden rage. Kevin typically laughed his problems away.

"Stop trying to overanalyze my feelings. I'm mad because my dad had an affair."

"What? When did you find this out?"

"It's in the book!"

I rubbed my temples. "Kevin, the book isn't a biography."

"Listen to me," Kevin said, his mouth full. "I'd heard my parents fighting before. My mom had accused him of sleeping around with tenants. I was young, and I didn't think too much of it because who *doesn't* sleep with their tenants?"

I raised my hand.

"In the book, Enst McMall was a womanizer who slept with both the women and *men*."

"You don't know that it's true," I said.

"Wait a second!" I started to put two and two together. "You think your dad had an affair with the roommates from El Salvador?"

"Between the book and the argument my parents had? Sure. He accused me of being immoral when he was the most immoral of us all!"

Reena hadn't mentioned Ernest McMills having an affair with the women in Apartment 11A. However, I didn't ask. We'd never talked about the women from El Salvador. My mind worked to make sense of this. Which was hard to do, given the fact it was midnight. There was still the screaming woman with a limp from Apartment 14B. I had no idea how she factored into this. "Do you think your dad had an affair with Larissa?"

"Who?"

"Honestly, do you listen to anything I say to you?"

"Every few words. You talk a lot."

I sucked in a breath and started, "Larissa is Lara and…you're not listening to me." His eyes were practically rolled up into his head.

"When you start a sentence with a big gulp of air, I know it's going to take *forever*."

I smacked my forehead. "We think the woman in the barrel is Larissa Lopez who disappeared in 1978. She was in a relationship with a married man…" I had to speak to Reena again. It was late, but the party had been just getting started when we left. There was a good chance she was up.

If only I had her phone number.

Wait one minute.

I may not have her phone number, but I did have book blogger Nathan's business card! Surely he still had to be at the party.

I dug my jeans out of the hamper and found the card still in the back pocket. Occasionally I amazed myself at how resourceful I could be. On the back of the card, it had Nathan's Snapchat, Facebook, Instagram, Litsy, Pinterest, Twitter, Tumblr, QQ, LinkedIn, Reddit, YouTube, Vine, Flixr, and

TikTok accounts. Along with his blog, website, email address, and *no* phone number.

No phone number!

How in the world could this man have every single social media account but not have a phone number? Honestly!

I went to Snapchat, Facebook, and Instagram and sent him a message with my phone number, asking him to call me ASAP. That it was a matter of life or death. Not a total exaggeration. We *did* have a dead person.

"What if he doesn't check his social media until tomorrow?" Kevin asked.

"Something tells me Nathan checks his accounts regularly."

"Why do you say that?"

"Because I can see he has already read my Facebook and Instagram messages. *Aaannnddd*, my phone is ringing." As soon as I answered, I could hear the music in the background. Hallelujah! The party was still going on. "Nathan, I have to speak to Reena Hike right now."

"Who is this?"

"I met you a few hours ago. You spoke to my friends Amy and Kevin. Is Reena there? It's an urgent matter. Tell her it's Cambria, and it's manager to manager. She'll know what that means."

"Sure, let me find her." I could hear the hesitation in his voice. The music became muffled, and I could hear indistinct chatter in the background.

"Who is this?" Reena demanded.

"It's Cambria Clyne. Sorry to bother you—I have a very important question. Did Ernest McMills have affairs with the residents?"

There was a beat of silence. "Go away," I heard her say to Nathan. A door closed and the music stopped. "What did you say?"

"Manager to manager, did Ernest McMills have affairs with his residents? It's in your book. Was that based on a true event?"

"Manager to manager, I don't know. I never witnessed anything. There were rumors of him spending *way* too much time in certain apartments."

"Do you know which apartments?"

"Not sure. One of the rumors I heard was that Mrs. McMills found out about his affairs, and that's one of the reasons they hired the management company and Trevor. So he wouldn't need to come around."

Kevin waved to get my attention. *Ask if my dad is gay*, he mouthed. I had Reena on speaker. I'd made Kevin promise not to say a word. Since this was *manager* to *manager* and all.

"What about him having affairs with men, too?" I asked Reena.

"I added that part to give the character depth. He was too dull as he was. Plus, I needed him to end up with the Czar of Thombadioan in the next book. It's the only way to insure the Civil War can commence."

Kevin pulled at his hair, red in the cheeks. "Spoiler alert," he angry whispered.

I gave him a look of warning, and he settled down. "Reena," I said, "the woman you saw arguing with Patrick, do you think she was a resident at one of the other properties the McMillses owned?"

"That could explain how she knew Patrick. He took over the entire McMills Los Angeles County portfolio."

Huh? That would put a wrench in my Larissa theory. This woman who went by Lara with the black pants could have been a resident from a different property. Maybe even the one I lived at. Mrs. McMills could have found out about the affair. Then she hired a management company, the woman found out she was pregnant, the woman tried to get in contact with Ernest McMills, Patrick told her no...

However.

Surely the medical examiner would have noted the woman was pregnant. So there goes that theory. She could have already had the baby, but what does that have to do with Sherman? Unless it was in fact Larissa and she'd had the baby back when she disappeared in 1978. Ernest McMills could have known about the pregnancy and thrown a bunch of money at her to make her disappear! She'd come back eighteen years later to…I wasn't sure. Tell Ernest McMills the child wanted to meet him? She first stopped at Sherman's apartment, since they were old friends. Then she came back, and that's when she ran into Patrick. She asked to get in touch with Ernest McMills—Patrick said no. Mr. McMills caught wind that she was in town, and he didn't want to risk his wife finding out about the kid, so he killed her.

However.

That would mean there's a love child out there in their early forties who was… My eyes slid to Kevin.

"Reena, I gotta go." I hung up the phone and asked Kevin, "What year were you born?"

"1978. Why are you making that face?"

Oh. No. No. No. No.

"You're not going to start crying again, are you?" Kevin asked. "You know I hate when you cry."

"Kevin," I said, trying to keep my voice calm.

"You don't think—" I started to say, fully questioning if I should even throw out this accusation.

"Not typically. But sometimes. Why?"

"I meant…" I sucked in a breath then quickly blew it out, not wanting to lose Kevin. "Do you think it's possible that your father had an affair with Larissa, she got pregnant, they hid her away, and she had the baby. Then your father raised that baby with your mother, and they…I don't know, paid this woman off. Then she reappeared when the child was eighteen, wanting to see him."

Kevin polished off his cereal. "I don't have any siblings. Remember?" He walked his bowl to the kitchen and dumped it in the sink.

"I wasn't talking about a sibling. I was talking about *you.*"

Kevin picked at his back teeth. "Start your story over. I forgot to listen to most of it."

Oh, for heaven's sake! I retold my theory, making sure Kevin paid attention this time.

"You don't think my mother was my mother?" he asked.

"It's a farfetched theory. Worth looking into, though. Do you have your birth certificate by chance?"

"Do you honestly think my parents would not put their names on the certificate if your crazy story were true?"

"No, but it should have the doctor's name, hospital, and place of birth. We could start there. You did say your mother never showed any affection towards you."

Kevin's mouth went to a line, and his eyes grew distant. He looked like he wanted to punch something again. I was out of giant stuffed animals. I did have a few throw pillows I didn't love.

"We need to find out. Let's go," he said.

"Whoa, where are you going?"

"To get my birth certificate. Grab your shoes."

"Whoa, whoa, whoa. Where is your birth certificate?"

"At my parents' house."

"Whoa, whoa, whoa. You want to go to your parents' house in the middle of the night?"

"Yeah. You coming?"

"Whoa, whoa, whoa. We could request the certificate from the state."

Kevin gave me a look, as if my stupidity had offended him. "That will take months. Are you coming or not?"

"Um…" I wrestled with the decision. See, I was trying this new thing where I didn't intentionally insert myself into dangerous situations. And it was quite possible that Ernest McMills was a killer.

Ultimately I said, "Let me change first." Because I was also trying this new thing where I kept Kevin out of jail. And he was less likely to break any laws if I was around.

CHAPTER EIGHTEEN

Proficient at fighting fires
(both figuratively and literally)

The McMillses lived in Brentwood—a quiet, upscale neighborhood in Los Angeles near the Getty Museum. The streets were lined with trees. The houses were large, and the movie stars were plentiful. Even in the dead of the night, the mansions were stunning, each one lovelier than the next. Until we reached 2256 East Vincent Street.

Situated between a Mediterranean style home with a well-groomed yard, and an Italian style home with vines crawling up the sides, sat a massive clunker of a house with dead grass, and chipped paint.

I slowed down and peered out the window of my car. "This is where you grew up?"

"Yep. The man refused to fix anything, and looks like he's stuck to his mantra."

"Don't they have an HOA?"

"Yep, and they hate him."

"I can't believe the HOA hasn't done something about this."

Kevin shrugged. "Ernest and *Enest* don't part with money easily."

"So I've heard. But they do have a yacht?"

"My mom inherited it when her mother died. She's the one who came from money."

"And your dad is the one who is cheap?"

"They're both cheap. Park down the street."

I pulled over in front of a house with a high fence and crawled out of my car. "What is your plan?" I asked Kevin as we hiked back up the street.

"I'm going to ring the doorbell."

"OK."

"Then I'm going to ask for my birth certificate."

"OK."

"And if they don't give it to me, I'm going to ask if my dad had an affair."

"OK."

"And if he says no, then I'm going home."

"Oh. OK." Seemed a bit anticlimactic. It also didn't sound illegal. Looked like Kevin didn't need me there after all.

"Then I'm going to smash a brick through their window."

I spoke too soon.

The driveway was long, with weeds towering from the cracks in the cement. Kevin stepped up to the door, and I hung back.

"What are you doing?" he asked.

"You want me to be part of this conversation?"

He jerked his head, as if to say, *Duh.*

Alrighty then. I stepped behind him, my phone in hand, ready to dial for help should the situation go south.

Kevin bypassed the old-fashioned lion-head knocker on the front door and pounded with the inside of his fists. A second-story window illuminated, and a few minutes later, the front porch light turned on.

A thin, tall man with droopy cheeks and gray hair opened the door and tightened his robe. "Kevin?"

"Hello, old man. I need my birth certificate."

Wow, he was sticking to his plan.

Mr. McMills' mouth sagged open, and his eyes shifted to me. "Who is that?"

"It's my wife," Kevin said.

I raised my hand, about to protest, then thought better of it.

"Wife?" Mr. McMills' face was plagued with confusion. "You married her?"

"Yeah, I know. Her hair is wild, and she talks a lot. She's good company, though."

Honestly.

"I need my birth certificate," Kevin said again. "Now."

"You can order one from the county," Mr. McMills said.

"No, I want it from you. I'm sure it's here somewhere." He pushed past his father and into the home.

I moseyed on forward, keeping enough distance to not be in the way yet close enough to still hear what was going on.

"You can't come barging into this house." Mr. McMills' words were harsh, though his tone was light. "Your mother is sleeping."

Kevin spun around. "*Is* she my mother?"

Mr. McMills scowled. "Of course she is."

"Did you hear about the woman in the barrel?"

"Yes, Trevor told us. Very sad. I don't see what that has to do with us."

"You don't, *Enest*?"

"Are you high?" Mr. McMills ran his hand down his face. "Don't make me call the police, Kevin. Just go back home."

"He's been sober for nine months," I said, then stepped back and assumed my position at the door.

"The little woman is right. Sober nine months," said Kevin. "No thanks to you."

Mr. McMills closed his eyes, as if counting to ten. "Kevin, please leave."

"No. I want my birth certificate."

"Why?"

"Because I think you are *immoral*."

Mr. McMills tensed. "You don't know what you're talking about."

"Did you have an affair with a woman named Marisa Lola?"

Oh, geez. I raised my hand. "Sorry to interrupt. I think he means Larissa Lopez. She also went by Lara." I took a step back, then remembered. "By the way, we think Larissa is the woman dead in the barrel."

Mr. McMills' face blanched. So much so I questioned his involvement in Larissa's death. If he'd killed her and stuffed her into the barrel, then he wouldn't have looked as if this was the first time he was hearing the news. Or he was a good actor. Or he blanched because he knew he'd been caught.

"Get out!" Mr. McMills pointed to the door. "Get out of my house, now! You are not welcome here." He grabbed Kevin by the arm and forced him forward. "Take your wife and leave."

"Such a hothead, old man," Kevin said, dragging his feet.

"Get out of my house!" He gave Kevin one hard push and slammed the door closed.

Well, oh, em, gee. I rocked from my toes to my heels, unsure of what to say next.

Kevin started laughing. "Did you see his face? He was all"—Kevin puffed his cheeks —"*get out of my house.*"

"Yeah, I saw. He absolutely knew Larissa."

"Ha! What a wacko." He sighed with a big smile on his face. "OK, cool. I'm good. Let's go."

"You didn't get your certificate," I said.

"So?"

"And you don't have answers."

"So?"

"Don't you want to know what happened?"

"Nah. I'm good." He shrugged. "Let's go. Jack in the Box is open twenty-four hours."

"Wait a second." I grabbed Kevin by the sleeve of his shirt. "*Larissa* could have been your mother."

"Then she's dead, and it doesn't matter. I want a taco."

"How can you not care?"

"Why do you?" he retorted. "This isn't your family. This isn't your life. The only reason you're doing any of this is because you want the job at Cedar Creek. You don't give a crap about what happened to anyone."

My breath hitched in my throat. I specifically hadn't told Kevin about my interview next door. "How'd you find out?"

"I saw you sneaking over there wearing your blue dress and put two and two together."

"It's a good opportunity," I said, feeling guilty.

"Listen to my words," he said, as if he were about to explain something very simple to someone very stupid. "All I care about right now is a deep-fried taco. You can work wherever. Marry whoever. Eat whatever. Dress however. I don't care so long as you don't cry."

"It's *whom*," I muttered. "And why do you have to be so mean? Sure, you had a crap family who did crap things in this crap house. I have done nothing but be there for you since day one...well, more like day seven or eight. You were a belligerent butthead in the beginning, but whatever."

Kevin looked up and mouthed *why* to the sky.

"What are you doing?" I demanded.

"Sometimes it's easier to care about tacos, than to think about the stuff you can't change." He gestured to the house.

Oh.

"I'm sure your boyfriend and his partner with the ugly hair will figure this out without us," Kevin added.

Perhaps.

"What we *can* do is get into your car, drive to Jack in the Box, eat two tacos, curly fries, and a vanilla shake, take five Tums, and go to bed."

Not a terrible plan. But, "I want chocolate."

"Gah! You're so difficult." He playfully wrapped his arm around my shoulders and pulled me into his armpit. "By the way, you're paying."

"Then it's only one taco."

"When you get the new job, you'll need to start buying better groceries. I'm sick of your generic, non-dairy, foo-foo garbage."

"First, it's cheaper. Second, Lilly has a milk allergy."

"According to WebMD."

"Your point?"

"How many hours a day do you spend on the website?"

"Not relevant." *A lot.* "You could buy your own food."

"New subject. Let's talk about Hampton's hair. I think we should stage an intervention."

"Guess who has to go to dinner with him and Silvia on Fri—"

An explosion cut me off. Kevin and I whirled around, using our hands to protect our face from the heat radiating off the McMills's McMansion. Flames spewed from a second-story window and up to the roof.

"No!" Kevin ran towards the house before I could stop him.

"Wait, Kevin!" I chased after him.

He kicked the door, but it didn't open. "This…looks…so…much…easier…in…the…movies," he said with each kick.

I pulled my shirt up to cover my nose and mouth and reached over and tried the handle. It was unlocked, and the door swung open. The entryway was filled with smoke, and about seven houses' worth of stuff. Oh, my gosh. I could see into the living room, and there were manmade hallways through piles of flammable-looking books and clothes and artifacts and furniture. This was an arsonist's dream.

Kevin headed up the spiral staircase, taking two steps at a time. For someone who hated his parents, he sure was eager to save them. I went after him, fumbling with my phone, wanting to call 9-1-1, but I dropped it on the floor. The thick smoke made it impossible to see where it had gone, and I decided to keep going. The explosion had been loud. A neighbor would have called for help already.

I followed Kevin down a hallway lined with more stuff and into a room. The smoke was getting thicker by the second, and I hunched down. "Kevin, we need to get out of here," I yelled out, my voice hoarse.

I had no idea what room we were in, and I had lost sight of Kevin. A little disoriented, I spun around, and stepped forward. Loud voices caught my attention, and I followed the sound. The smoke cleared with each step, and I found myself at the end of a hallway. The door was half shut (or half open for the optimist, not that there was anything optimistic about this situation). Inside, Mr. McMills and a woman who I assumed to be Mrs. McMills were arguing. She had a gun in one hand and lighter fluid in the other. They were in what appeared to be a library, with shelves stuffed with dusty—flammable-looking—books.

"I had no choice, Ernest!" she yelled.

"Stop it, Dolores. Put the gun down."

"Put it down?" Dolores mocked. She had a helmet of bleached hair, a tight face, and red nails. A silk robe was wrapped around her bony frame, and yesterday's makeup was still caked on her face. "You want me to put the gun down?" She fired two shots into the bookshelf. "Who is the one who couldn't keep it in his pants?"

"I-I understand," Mr. McMills said, backing up, his palms up. "Just put the gun down."

"She wanted the kid, and I *dealt* with it."

"Please, put the gun down."

Dolores fired another shot into a stack of books. "I'm the one who had to look your infidelity in the face every day!"

"You never told me Larissa came back."

"Because you would have let her see the boy!" She waved the gun around. "I should have listened to my parents. They told me you were no good."

I coughed as silently as I could into the crook of my elbow, not wanting to be heard. It sounded to me as if I was right. Larissa was pregnant with Mr. McMills' baby, but it was *Dolores* who put Larissa in the barrel, and I wanted to hear more.

Also, Dolores appeared to be unstable, and I wasn't eager to get caught in the crossfire. The problem was the actual fire was inching its way closer. I'd soon have no choice but to join them in the room. I crouched down to the floor where the air was cleaner, and listened.

"I didn't know you killed her," Mr. McMills said. "Why did you kill her, Dolores?"

"I had no choice. She wanted to see the kid. That was part of the deal. She was never to see him. Don't you understand, you idiot? She would have made things worse!"

"But you *killed* her."

"No one was supposed to find the body," she said.

My heart pounded and my mind scrambled. Despite the alarming amount of carbon monoxide in the air, I was able to make sense of the situation. Ernest had had an affair with Larissa, and she'd gotten pregnant. Dolores and Ernest paid her off and told her to stay away, kept the baby themselves, and raised him as their own. When Larissa didn't keep her end of the bargain, Dolores killed her, likely in a heated argument, by smacking her on the back of the head with something heavy. I wasn't sure how little Dolores managed to get a dead body up to the attic, into a barrel, and construct a wall by herself. But desperate people manage to do desperate things all the time.

Patrick must have known about Kevin—that's why he'd been acting so strange. Larissa must have told him the truth when the two were arguing.

Hallelujah, my boss is innocent! I felt like singing. Except I was running out of oxygen. I only hoped Kevin had found whatever it was he was looking for and had managed to escape.

Speaking of escape... The fire raged forward, and I was left with no other option. I crawled into the room, hoping the dueling duo wouldn't notice.

"Who the hell is that?" Dolores spit out.

So, I guess my plan was a bust.

"That's Kevin's wife," Mr. McMills said.

"Wife?" Dolores took a staggering step back, and I took note of her limp. She must have been the woman who came by Apartment 14B today. She heard about the barrel and went to see for herself if it had been discovered. So it wasn't a ghost.

I stood up slowly, my hands up and shaking. I could not believe I was in this situation. I'd come to make sure Kevin didn't do anything stupid, and here I was on the wrong side of a gun— again!

Note to self: Time to reevaluate your life choices.

"You're Kevin's wife?" Dolores didn't hide the shock from her voice. She still held the gun and lighter fluid tightly in each hand.

"Errr..." I wasn't sure what to say.

So Kevin said it for me.

He fell into the room, coughing, his face covered in soot. "I got it." He held up a handful of records. "My"—*cough, cough, cough*—"Barbara Streisand collection," he gasped out. "I found it."

Oh, for heaven's sake.

"Kevin!" Dolores's voice shook. "What are you doing here?"

He looked at the records in his hand then at his mother and shrugged, as if it were obvious.

"You're...m-married?" she stuttered.

Kevin coughed into the inside of his elbow and nodded his head. "This is my ball...and...chain." He smacked my butt.

Oh, geez.

Dolores shook her head. "You told us you were gay."

"Yeah, well, you told me"—he paused to cough—"that you were my mother."

"I *am* your mother," she said with a stomp of her foot. "What are you talking about?"

"No," he coughed, "Mari…or…Lar…" He looked down at me. "What was her name?"

"Larissa," I muttered.

"Larissa was my mother!"

"No, she was not!" Dolores waved her gun around, and I cowered behind Kevin, my shirt still over my nose and mouth.

"Kevin, what are you talking about?" Mr. McMills asked. "This is your mother. She was pregnant—" He stopped himself.

"What?" Kevin demanded. "Get out with it, old man. We're all going to die here anyway."

Uh, I'm not dying.

I hoped.

Dolores fired another shot into the bookcase. "Keep your mouth quiet," she warned her husband.

Mr. McMills' eyes were approaching frantic. "I'm tired of lying!" He crossed the room and put a hand on Kevin's shoulder. "I had an affair with a *beautiful* Latina girl from El Salvador. You were our love child."

"You've"—Kevin coughed—"got to be kidding me!"

"Your mother couldn't have kids," Mr. McMills continued. "She has low libido. You were our chance to be parents. We paid Larissa to go away and let us raise you. For what it's worth, I think we did a terrible job."

Kevin blinked a few times, the Barbara Streisand collection still in his hands. "You killed my real mom?"

Mr. McMills brought a hand to his heart. "Your mother did. She's ashamed of my affairs. It's not my fault. I have needs."

Oh, please make it stop.

The way Mr. McMills' mouth curved into a faint smile when he said *needs* made me shudder. It's like I was trapped in a telenovela with a pervy grandpa.

"Seriously?" Kevin gasped. The smoke billowed in, and I kicked the door closed to buy us time.

"It has taken every ounce of power I have to keep your father from ruining our name!" Dolores fired another shot into the ceiling. Chunks of drywall fell down, and we all covered our heads.

I checked around for the nearest exit. The only window was behind Dolores. We had to get the gun away from her and make a break for it.

"Dolores, I don't see how burning the house down will serve any purpose," Mr. McMills said. "Put the gun down."

"No!" She doused the shelf behind her with lighter fluid. "If I'm going down, you're going down with me. I will not spend the rest of my life in prison because of you."

Great. If she fired a shot, this room would go up in flames. Just in case it didn't, she dropped the lighter fluid and produced a lighter.

"Stop!" I jumped out from behind Kevin. "You can't do this. You'll kill us all."

Dolores could not have cared less. I knew because she said, "I couldn't care less."

"I'm a-a mother," I stuttered. "I have a child. She needs me."

Dolores faltered. "I have a grandchild?"

No, but, sure. Let's go with it. "She's three, and she's beautiful. She has big hazel eyes, curly hair, and a sweet, heart-shaped face. Right now, she loves Captain Marvel and anything to do with unicorns. She just started preschool, and she's obsessed with her daddy...*Kevin*." I hoped to tug on Dolores's heartstrings. "I need to be there for my kid. Please, *please*, don't kill me."

Without uttering a word, she jerked her head to the window. I shuffled towards her with my hands up in the air. There was a single moment of hesitation when I passed her. My eyes went to the gun and lighter in her shaking hands. I knew she had a slight limp and wasn't in the right frame of mind. It wouldn't take much to tackle her to the ground. Seemed like a no-brainer, but then there was Lilly to think about, and my promise to Chase to be careful. Leaving was the only surefire way to escape this situation alive.

The thing was, though, I couldn't have *lived* with myself if I'd left. Not if something happened to Kevin. With slow determination, I unlocked the window and pushed it open. The plan was to catch Dolores off guard and rush her once she thought I was gone.

I climbed up on the shelf below the window. My body pumped adrenaline, ready to attack, when Dolores shoved me with all her might. I rolled down an awning and landed in a bush. I stumbled to my feet and limped to the front of the house. *Kevin!*

A group of neighbors had already gathered on the sidewalk. Someone pulled me away from the burning building as I protested each step, screaming for Kevin. He was inside. He was inside!

A man with a shaved head and goatee held me by the shoulders to keep me from running in. This felt like a dream. A really bad dream. As if I were outside of my body watching the entire event from above: the fire trucks pulling up one by one; the police cars quickly following; the firefighters with gas masks and oxygen strapped to their backs, filing into the house, dragging a hose.

I clasped my hands and pleaded with God or whomever would listen to please, please let Kevin be OK. But as the fire died down and the first responders emerged empty-handed, my hope dwindled. There was no way anyone could have survived. The house was charred.

With nothing better to do, I shouted for help. I shouted until a police officer approached to ask me if I was all right.

I was covered in soot, my voice was hoarse, and my friend was in the house. Of course I was not *all right!*

Which was exactly what I told the officer.

"How many people were in there?" she asked.

"Three! The McMillses and Kevin. You have to find Kevin!"

The police officer—a woman with a bun of dark hair—spoke into the radio on her shoulder and told me to please see the paramedic.

I'm not sure what happened next. Somehow, I ended up sitting in the back of an ambulance with an oxygen mask on. I should have taken Kevin to get his tacos right away. But *no*, I had to press, and press, and press, and press. Forcing him to care more than he did. All for what? Some stupid job? I didn't even want the job anymore!

Chase pushed his way through the crowd with Hampton hot on his tail. "Cambria!" He wrapped me in a hug, and I buried my head in his chest.

"Kevin," I rasped out. "Kevin was in the house."

Chase struggled to understand, and I removed the oxygen mask.

"Kevin was in the house," I repeated.

Chase lowered his head and squeezed his eyes shut. We stayed like that for a while, and held each other without uttering a word. I couldn't believe Kevin was gone.

When I'd first met him, he was high and naked and skinny-dipping. He called me names, slammed doors in my face, and promised to get me fired. Slowly, our relationship shifted. He'd come over for breakfast, and lunch, and dinner, and dessert, and midnight snacks. We'd stay up late watching *If Only*, our favorite crime show. We'd become friends. Best friends, even.

Then there was Vegas…oh, Vegas.

CHAPTER NINETEEN

—————

Balances family relations

I was transported to the hospital, where I was diagnosed with a sprained wrist and smoke inhalation, a diagnosis I could have given myself, considering it hurt to breathe and my wrist felt like it was about to fall off. It would have saved me the thousand-dollar hospital bill.

Chase rode with me. He dared not utter a word. I knew he wasn't happy that I'd—yet again—inserted myself into a dangerous situation. I also knew he wasn't going to say anything, not now, not with Kevin…

I lay there in a hospital bed with the oxygen mask strapped over my mouth and nose. It was a busy night in the ER. I could hear the labored breathing of the patient on the other side of the curtain that was pulled around my bed, the whispering of the nurses, the tapping of someone's long nails on their phone screen, and a symphony of coughing. Chase sat at the foot of the bed, silently studying his hands. I stared down at the ACE bandage wrapped around my wrist and moved my fingers, welcoming the pain that took my mind off Kevin for even a second.

The curtain flung open. It was Hampton with his hair on and pants hiked. He nodded to Chase, and Chase nodded back then rose to his feet and stepped into the hallway. I put my head back on the pillow and stared up at the tiled ceiling. Counting the little specs to keep my mind from circling around what had just transpired.

Chase touched my shoulder. "He's alive," he said.

He's alive!

I would have leapt from the bed if it weren't for the oxygen mask keeping me tethered.

"His mother pushed him out the window before the house went up," Chase said. "He's banged up, but he's going to be OK."

I had serious doubt that Kevin would be OK. Physically, maybe. Not emotionally. Not after all that had been revealed.

How could he be? There was no way.

* * *

OK, maybe I was wrong.

Once I was released, I went to Kevin, who was four beds down, right next to the ambulance entrance. His left arm hung in a sling, and there was a gauze bandage covering a burn on his shoulder. He had the goofiest grin on his face. I knew it wasn't the drugs. He'd told the nurse he was a recovering addict, and all they gave him was high doses of Motrin.

"I brought you tacos," I said and closed the curtain behind me. I'd had Chase run to Jack in the Box before I was released. "Two tacos and curly fries."

"Where's the shake?" His voice sounded as if he'd swallowed sandpaper.

"I forgot the shake. I'm sorry."

"Come on, Clyne. You had one job." He tried to sit up, and I stopped him.

"Rest."

"When do I get out of here?"

"The nurse said an hour or two. They're pretty busy. Your injuries aren't too bad, considering."

"Considering I fell from a burning building."

I took a seat on the foot of his bed. "I'm so sorry about your parents."

"I'm not. They were terrible, awful, dreadful, appalling people who died in a terrible fire in a terrible house, and they'll live terribly ever after."

"At least you have answers, right?"

"And tacos."

"And tacos."

"And Barbara Streisand." His mouth curved into a weak smile. "It's my one stereotypical gay man obsession."

"I can't believe you ran into a burning building to save the records."

"They're first editions. I'd been contemplating breaking into the house to grab them for years, but I didn't want to risk dealing with my parents," he said. "I *finally* got them back. Do you know how much money I could get for them? Should cover rent for a few months."

I couldn't help but laugh. "I'm glad you're not dead."

"Yeah, me too…ugh." He scowled.

"What's wrong? Do you need more medicine?"

"No, I'm just thinking about what Trevor will say when he finds out." He shoved his finger down his throat. "He is the most annoying human on the planet."

Right. That. I wondered how Trevor would take the news. Not well, I suspected.

* * *

So I was wrong again.

An hour later, Trevor arrived. I could smell him walking down the hall. He had a sage-lavender aroma. "Cousin!" He flung open the curtain.

Kevin tried to escape from the bed, but the IVs in his arm kept him from moving.

"And my favorite manager." Trevor kissed me on each cheek. "Come. Come." He pulled me closer to Kevin and placed his thumbs on our foreheads.

Kevin and I exchanged a look, unsure of what was happening. Trevor's eyes were closed, and he appeared to be concentrating *really* hard.

"There," he finally said. "I have healed you."

I didn't feel any better. If anything, I felt worse. Probably because Kevin could not have looked more miserable, and I could tell Trevor had been crying. How could he not? He'd found out that his aunt was a murderer, his uncle a playboy, and they both died in a big house fire his aunt had started. It was like an episode of *If Only.*

Except…if this were *If Only*, Mr. and Mrs. McMills would have miraculously emerged from the flames in a dramatic slow-motion shot and made amends with Kevin.

"I have spoken to the police," Trevor said. "They've filled me in on everything, and it all makes perfect sense. I knew there was a disturbance at the Burbank building. Now I know why I felt it so strongly." I was surprised how well Trevor was taking all this in. A little *too* well. I leaned in closer and took a whiff.

Well, that explained it. He was high as a kite. I could smell the pot on his breath. Not that I blamed him. There were worse coping mechanisms out there.

Speaking of which, I could have really gone for a gallon of ice cream and a seventy-two-hour nap.

Of course, the death of the McMillses made Trevor a multimillionaire. Not that money was everything. But nine figures in the bank could help soften the blow.

Trevor had Kevin's hand. "I'd always considered you ungrateful, neurotic, impulsive, crude—a black sheep with a negative aura—until I attended my energy workshop. After a seventy-two-hour fast, it came to me in a vision. You and I have to make amends."

"Oh, hell," Kevin mumbled under his breath.

CHAPTER TWENTY

Can make good decisions in high-pressure situations

Kevin was released from the hospital around sunrise. Trevor wanted to bring him back to his house, but Kevin said he'd rather "Die. Decease. Depart. Expire. Perish. Drink my own urine." So Chase and I brought him to my apartment.

Amy was up and sober and in the kitchen dropping two Alka-Seltzer into a cup of water when we walked in. She still had on last night's clothes, and makeup, and her hair resembled mine.

"Where have you been…" Amy's voice trailed off when she looked up. "Sheesh, what happened to you?"

"Rough night." Kevin walked past her and rummaged through the fridge until he found the last of the leftover pizza.

"Seriously, Kevin." Amy covered her nose. "You smell terrible, and why is your arm in a sling?"

"Cambria beat me," he said while attempting to remove a slice of pepperoni from the Ziploc with only one hand.

"No, I did not." I came around the counter and helped him with the pizza. Between the two of us, we had a pair of working hands. "How many slices?"

"Three."

"How are you even hungry?"

"Are _you_ seriously questioning _me_ about my stress-eating choices?"

True. I went ahead and warmed up four slices. Three for him. One for me.

"Can someone please tell me what is going on!" Amy winced at her own voice and sipped her Alka-Seltzer. "You two smell awful and look like crap. And what happened to the elephant? I woke up to find it ripped apart in the living room."

Chase walked into the kitchen and dropped my purse on the counter. "I can't believe you paid fifty bucks for that thing."

"*Yes.* I thought it was cute." Amy shuffled to the living room and slowly lowered herself onto the couch, tucking her leg under her bony little butt. "I feel like I missed something here."

I sat at the kitchen table with my pizza. I did not feel like recounting the night's events to Amy, but I knew I had to. I sucked in a breath, ready to tell the long tale. "We thought the woman in the—"

Kevin cut me off. "My dad had an affair with some woman named Lola Marissa something. They had a kid. It's me. My parents paid her to disappear. Lola Marissa Something came back. My mom killed her, shoved her into a barrel. When she found out that I knew, she burned the house down. The end."

I guess it wasn't as long of a tale as I thought.

Except, "The woman's name was Larissa Lopez."

"Tomayto. Tomahto."

"It's really not."

"Nothing has been confirmed," Chase said from the kitchen, helping himself to the last pizza slice.

"You don't think it was Zola?" Kevin asked.

"Honestly," I grunted. "It's Lola—I mean, *Larissa.*"

"It's Jane Doe," Chase corrected. "We have not confirmed anyone's identify yet."

Amy joined us at the kitchen table. "Wouldn't that be funny if it were someone totally different?"

"No!" Kevin, Chase, and I all said in unison.

"Fine then." Amy sipped her drink.

Chase sat across from me at the table, shaking his head. "I still can't believe you confronted the McMillses."

"It was his idea." I pointed to Kevin. "I only came to make sure he didn't do anything illegal. I never thought they'd burn the house down and Kevin would run in to save Barbara Streisand."

Amy almost spit out her drink. "Barbara Streisand was there?"

"Hell, no," Kevin said. "Babs is too good for the McMillses."

Amy sighed. "That is so true."

I stared down at my pizza, regretting my decision to consume greasy carbs before seven a.m. *Ugh.* "Where did you and Hampton go after you left my apartment?" I asked Chase.

"We made contact with Maria. She confirmed that Larissa had been having an affair with a married man. Larissa wouldn't tell Maria the name of the man, but she had her suspicions."

"That doesn't make sense," Kevin said. "We talked to Maria, and Cambria told her there was a dead chick in a barrel. Why didn't she mention her missing friend, Larissa?"

"It's Lar—" I started to correct then realized he'd said it right.

"Maria thought that Larissa got pregnant and took off," Chase said. "She didn't tell Larissa's aunt because she didn't want to bring shame to her family. Not sure how allowing her aunt to think that her niece had been kidnapped was any better. But this was a different era. Still, we don't know anything for sure. Not until it's been confirmed."

"How long will it take to confirm?" I asked.

Chase shrugged. I wasn't sure if he shrugged because he didn't know or because he didn't want to answer. He'd already given us more details than he probably should have.

"And we did get ahold of Patrick," Chase said. "He came down to the station with his lawyer. He did confirm that a woman named Larissa had come by looking for Sherman. She'd asked Patrick if he could contact the McMillses for her. Patrick called Dolores McMills, and she told Patrick to make Larissa go away. Patrick told Larissa to leave. Then Larissa launched into a story about how she'd gotten pregnant with Ernest's kid, Dolores found out, and paid her to disappear. Larissa was young and naïve, took the money, moved to Texas, got her act together, and returned when the child was eighteen. Patrick sent her away. Then, when Cambria found the woman in the barrel—"

"Fox found him," I interjected.

"When *Fox* found a woman in the barrel and she matched the description of Larissa, Patrick got nervous. He put two and two together, and worried he'd be a prime suspect since Dolores had specifically asked him to get rid of Larissa. Which is why he'd been reluctant to talk to us. His lawyer was out of town, and he returned late last night."

"Ha! He had nothing to do with her death," I said, sounding a little smug. I'd known Patrick's hands were clean. I mean...I'd basically known. Mostly. I may have had my doubts. Which was perfectly reasonable, given how strange he'd been acting since we found the barrel. Now I knew why. Except...

Ugh.

I'd forgotten about the whole job debacle.

"Hampton was in the interview when I received word that your car was at the McMills's house," Chase said.

"You tracked my car?" I asked.

"No, I should from now on. But we had the McMills's house under surveillance."

Oh. Made sense.

"Enough of all that." Amy brushed her hair over her shoulder. "Now that the murder nonsense is all taken care of, let's get back to the important stuff. I want proposal details."

Chase choked on his pizza. "You told...told...her?" He pounded on his chest with his fist to help the chunk of dough work its way down his esophagus.

"Of course she told me. She tells me everything," Amy said. "Also, I found the ring in her bag."

"Which one?" Kevin asked, and I kicked him under the table.

"Ouch! What did you do that for? I'm already banged up enough...oh." His face lit up with realization. "I mean which...*suitcase*...did...you...oh, hell. I'm too tired to think."

Amy turned to Chase. "Did you give her two rings? I personally love the one-carat, white gold, vintage, halo-style, channel-set, round diamond."

Chase scrunched his brows together. "Two?"

I was up on my feet taking my plate to the sink. Also, it seemed a good time to reorganize my condiment drawer. I had about fifty packs of Taco Bell sauces stashed in there.

"Are you talking about the ring Tom gave her?" Chase asked Amy.

Amy slapped a hand over her mouth then winced in pain and took a sip of her Alka-Seltzer. "Tom proposed, too."

"You didn't tell her?" Chase asked me.

"You told Chase?" Kevin asked me.

"Why didn't you tell me Tom proposed?" Amy asked me.

That was just a whole lot of questions for someone who was on mild painkillers with a sprained wrist, smoke in her lungs, and Taco Bell sauces to organize.

Kevin raised his uninjured hand. "Uh, I thought we were keeping Tom's proposal a secret from Chase?"

"Why would she keep that a secret from me?" Chase asked.

"*Because* we don't tell you everything about Tom, obviously."

Oh, hell. If looks could kill, Kevin would have been facedown in his pizza. Honestly!

"What is he talking about?" Chase asked me.

"Nothing. I told you about the proposal, and I told you about the kiss in the bathroom on my birthday."

Amy gasped. "Why did you tell him about the kiss?"

Chase moved his hands around helplessly, as if he were juggling imaginary balls. "We're dating. Of course she told me. Why do you want her to lie to me?"

"It's not a lie," Amy said. "It's an omission."

"I'm super confused as to what we're talking about," Kevin said, staring up at the ceiling. "I think I have a secondary high from Trevor."

That makes two of us.

Kevin snorted. "You know what would make this situation super awkward?"

"What?" Amy asked.

"If Tom and Lilly were to show up." Kevin pointed to the window.

Oh, no. I dropped my Taco Bell sauces on the floor and checked to see if Kevin was being hypothetical. Sure enough, there was Tom, strolling down the walkway in a gray fitted suit, white collared shirt, and black tie, hand-in-hand with Lilly, who was wearing an Iron Man costume. She was holding Munch's leash. Munch was Tom's dog. He was a scruffy little mutt who was as wide as he was long, and Tom treated him as if he were his second child. He currently had on a red harness, a UCLA bandana, and...shoes?

Kevin clapped. "This should be fun."

"Loads." Chase swigged the rest of Amy's Alka-Seltzer.

There was a knock on the door, and everyone stood up simultaneously, as if they'd been rehearsing their timing. I grabbed Kevin by the arm and yanked him into the kitchen. "Chase doesn't know about Vegas yet," I muttered.

"You said you told him," he whispered.

"Not about the wedding chapel, just about the proposal."

"Ooohhh, this is going to be good."

No, it's not.

And I had no plans to tell Chase in front of Tom, and Kevin, and Amy. I had plans to tell him privately. Later. Like before the end of the year.

I pushed past everyone and answered the door. "Hi. Give me." I pointed to Lilly's go-between bag swung over Tom's shoulder.

"Cam, what happened to your hand?"

"Minor sprain. Hurry!"

The door swung open. "Thomas Dryer." Amy crossed her arms. "You have some explaining to do."

Tom's eyes swiveled around, as if he were looking for the nearest exit.

"We aren't doing this now," I said and grabbed Lilly by the hand. "Did you have the best day ever at preschool?"

"Yes," she cheered. "I drew a picture, and painted a picture, and played blocks, and went down the slide, and colored a picture, and made a sandcastle, and counted bubbles, and..."

She continued for another two minutes. Tom, Chase, Amy, Kevin, and I all stood there with forced enthusiasm plastered on our faces, waiting for her to finish.

"...and sang a song, and blew bubbles, and my teacher tied my shoe, and I went on the swing, and then...and then...that's it." She smiled triumphantly.

"That sounds like the best day ever," I said and kissed her on the top of her head.

"Ways better than showing apartments," she said.

True.

Tom removed his sunglasses. "Did I interrupt an intervention?"

"Yes!" Amy grabbed ahold of his tie and pulled him inside. Munch tottered behind, and I sneezed. I loved that dog. My allergies, not so much. "We need to hash out what happened in New York," Amy said then looked down at Lilly. "How about you go play in your room for just a little bit, kiddo."

Lilly scowled. "Why is hes here?" She pointed to Chase.

I shot Tom a look, and he held up his palms as if to say *it wasn't me*. "Lilly, sweetie." I bent down. "Why don't you want Chase around?"

Lilly shoved her fingers in her mouth. "Because I don't want him to knock yous up like the woman in the barrel."

There was a collective "ahhh, makes sense" sigh from four out of five adults in the room. I didn't sigh. I cringed, and died a little inside.

"Sweetie, you don't have to worry about Chase ever hurting me. No one is getting knocked on the head."

She looked at me with her big hazel eyes, and my heart swelled. "Are you sure?"

"I promise. Chase is a policeman. Remember? He keeps the bad guys away."

"And Daddy gets them out of jail," she added.

"Falsely accused," Tom added then knelt down beside Lilly and tapped the tip of her nose. "I'd never let anyone hurt Mommy either. You don't need to worry."

Lilly thought this over, her fingers still shoved in her mouth.

"Got it?" Tom tickled her tummy. "Huh?"

She burst out into a laugh and turned to Chase. "You better not ever knock up my mommy, got it?" she said with a stern shake of her finger.

Oh, hell.

I massaged my temples.

"Got it." Chase gave her a high five, and she pranced out of the room, down the hall, and slammed her door shut. I knew that slam. It meant she was about to do a costume change. We didn't have much time. Thank goodness.

"OK." I paused to sneeze. "Glad that is taken care of. You should be on your way to work." I manually turned Tom by the shoulders and gave him a little shove.

"Not so fast." Amy blocked the door. "Please tell me what happened. I need to know if I'm planning a wedding or not."

The room fell silent.

Ugh.

Fine!

I sucked in a breath. "After the show, Chase and I—"

"He took her to dinner and proposed," Kevin cut me off. "Cambria went, *'Ahhhh!'* and punched Chase in the face."

"That is not how it happened," Chase said. "She got excited and accidentally hit me in the eye with the ring."

Amy frowned. "So there was no fight?"

"No," I said and turned to Tom. "Don't you have work?"

He picked up Munch. "Nah, I'm good."

"Before we continue," said Amy, "can you please explain why your dog is wearing shoes?"

Tom peered down at Munch's feet, as if he hadn't noticed. "The cement is hot on his paws."

Chase and I exchanged a look, and he winked at me. He was awfully good-natured for having to deal with my intrusive friends and meddling baby daddy. Of course, he didn't know the whole truth.

"Anyway," Amy said. "Chase, why did you propose to Cambria? You two haven't been together that long."

"Because I love her and want to spend forever together."

Good answer.

"Awww." Amy clasped her hands and brought them to her cheek. "That's so sweet. But I call bull. You proposed because you're getting ready to leave for FBI training and you're worried Tom will swoop in while you're gone."

"No, I'm not," Chase said, unmoving.

"OK, so Chase proposes, Cambria says yes, punches him in the face, and then what happened?" Amy looked at Kevin.

"I didn't punch him in the face," I said. "Also, it's getting awfully late. I have a lot to do today, as I suspect both Chase and Tom do—"

"She changed her mind," Kevin said. "She was worried it was too soon to get engaged."

Gah!

I'd told him that in confidence.

We were in New York, and I'd gone to his room to show off my ring. At the time, I was beyond euphoric. I loved Chase. I couldn't imagine spending my life with anyone else. As soon as I'd flashed my one-carat diamond to Kevin, doubt began to slither its way into my head. Sure, I was twenty-nine years old, but was I ready for marriage? Were we—Chase and I—ready for marriage? Those questions had popped into my head, no matter how hard I'd tried to make them go away. The next morning, I'd told Chase I wanted time to think about it. That I didn't want to break up, of course, but I wasn't sure if it was the right time to get engaged, with him leaving soon for training.

"As soon as Cambria told me they were engaged, I knew it was time to take things to the next level," Tom said.

I sneezed.

"After Chase left, Cambria was a total downer," said Kevin. "Which is why I made the decision to cut our vacation short and go to Vegas. I also made the decision to text Tom and tell him what had happened and where we'd be." He turned to Chase. "Sorry, I'm Team Tom. He was my lawyer."

"Wait." Amy shook her head. "I thought Tom went to New York—that's why Lilly had the Statue of Liberty doll."

"It's the Statue of Liberty in Vegas," Tom said.

"Wow." Amy waved a hand. "Plot twist."

"So Tom showed up." Kevin sat on the couch and crossed his legs. "He proposed. Cambria punched him. He dislocated his shoulder."

That was a pretty accurate synopsis. Kevin and I had been walking through the lobby of the Bellagio when I'd spotted Tom approaching. I'd had to blink a few times to make sure my eyes weren't deceiving me. He'd had on light-washed jeans and a tight blue shirt, with a messenger bag hung over his shoulder. His hair had been a mess, and he'd had a scruffy jawline. He'd looked like a walking Abercrombie & Fitch mannequin.

Tom had approached us and grabbed me by the shoulders. "Don't marry him," he'd said. "I told you that I love you and I want to spend my life with you, and I meant every word." He'd reached into his pocket to retrieve the ring. It had taken him a minute since his pants were tight. When he'd managed to wrangle the little box out, he'd revealed the solitaire ring. It wasn't as glitzy as Chase's, not that I'd cared what the ring looked like. I'd cared more about the man holding it.

My first instinct had been to slap him. So I had. Right across the face, and he'd fallen back into a slot machine and dislocated his shoulder. We'd spent the next five hours in an emergency room. And if you've never been to a Las Vegas emergency room, let me tell ya, it's quite eye-opening.

The entire wait, he'd continued to profess his feelings. "I've loved you since the moment Lilly was born," he'd said. "I was too afraid to screw it up, so I put you off. The biggest regret of my life. I should have asked you to marry me then." The doctor had arrived, put his shoulder back in place, given him a sling, and sent us on our way. When we had reached the parking lot, I'd told him, "I can't marry you, Tom. Not now. Maybe not ever." He'd asked me to reconsider and encouraged me to keep the ring.

"That's it?" Amy asked. "Chase proposed, you said yes. Then you said you'd have to think about it. Then Tom proposed, and you said no." She frowned. "Anticlimactic. No?"

"Oh, but there's more," Kevin said, and I sent him a mental message to shut his mouth. He didn't get it. "Tom flew home with his injured arm, and Cambria was an even bigger downer. So we got drunk."

Amy cringed. "Nothing good happens when Cambria drinks."

Nope.

"We had a great time," Kevin said. "We went to a Magic Mike show. She got called up to the stage. She almost got arrested for swimming in the fountain at the Bellagio."

"You jumped into the fountain?" Tom asked.

"Not the big fountain outside the shows," I said. "He's talking about the little one in the lobby."

Chase covered his mouth to hide a smile.

"After I convinced the security guards to let Cambria go with a warning, we went to a bar at Circus Circus to refuel,"

Kevin said, and I dropped my head into my hands. "She was crying about what a giant mess her life was. How she had these two men who loved her. *Blah. Blah. Blah. Yada. Yada. Yada.* We got married, and Cambria bought me a thesaurus as a wedding gift."

Chase flinched, as if he'd just been slapped. "You did what?"

"She bought, purchased, procured, attained a thesaurus because she said I needed to learn words. I don't know. She was drunk."

"Hold on!" I fought back the panic. "There is far more to this story."

"Ugh." Kevin rested his head back on the couch. "You tell the longest stories," he moaned.

Amy was shaking her head. "You married Kevin?"

"Just listen to me—"

"I'm going to work." Chase strode across the living room in three large steps and swung open the front door.

I went after him. "Chase, wait!"

"I have work to do, Cambria." He dug his keys out of his pocket.

Mickey, my upstairs neighbor, marched by, muttering something about government conspiracies and corrupt cops. Both Chase and I stopped to say hello, then kept going.

"Chase, please let me explain." I followed him into the carports.

"Enough is enough, Cambria." He unlocked his car. "I asked you to marry me because I thought we were *there*. You wanted time to think about it, but went ahead and married Kevin on a whim, and didn't even bother to tell me."

"Please. Just listen to me."

Chase came to an abrupt halt, and I rammed into him, not expecting him to stop. "Go ahead. Explain," he said.

I started to suck in a breath, and then thought better of it. Chase was not in the mood for a long, drawn-out, Cambria explanation. I could tell by the look on his face.

"I was confused. OK. I want to marry you, but I wasn't sure we were ready. Then Tom showed up. He's Lilly's dad, so of course his proposal shook me. But, like I said, I told him no."

The morning after Kevin's and my nuptials, I'd woken in a panic, booked a flight, come home, gone straight to Chase's house, and told him everything. I'd told him about the kiss Tom and I shared in the bathroom on my birthday. I'd told him how Tom had confessed his feelings to me a couple of weeks earlier. I'd told him that Tom had shown up with a ring and asked me to marry him. "I can't compete with him," Chase had said. "It's a losing battle. If you want to be with him, be with him. I get it. No judgment. Stop stringing me along." His words had been like little daggers to my heart. I'd realized in that moment that what I was doing to Chase was what Tom had done to me for so many years. He was on his own emotional roller coaster with me. The thought was *horrid*. I'd decided in that moment to give him my full heart. Even if I didn't accept his proposal, I had said that I would save the ring for when we were ready.

I should have told him about Kevin.

In my defense, I didn't remember too much about the night.

Chase was growing impatient, and people were starting to file out of their apartments and to their carports. I did not want to have a fight with my boyfriend in front of my residents. But I didn't want to lose my boyfriend either. "I was drunk. I was so unbelievably drunk and upset and crying...a lot. I'm not sure why we decided to get married, but I'm like ninety-nine percent positive that we didn't sign the marriage certificate."

"I can't even—"

"Don't say can't," I cut him off. "It's been a really, *really* hard year. And I am a terrible decision maker, which is why I don't drink. At least you know that there's nothing going on between Kevin and me. It was a mistake. I'm so sorry."

Chase clenched his jaw and looked heavenward. "I got my orders," he said.

Oh, no. My heart clenched. I knew he'd be sent off for training, but I still wasn't ready for him to go. "Where and when?"

"Quantico in Virginia, and I leave in two weeks."

I nodded, feeling the effects of the last twenty-four hours with the fire, and attack by an author in pleather, and falling out of a second-story window, and solving a murder, and finding out

I was jobless. I massaged the back of my neck, working out a kink. "I'll be here for you when you get back from training," I said to him, and I meant it. "You don't have to worry."

Chase studied me intensely, and I worked hard to not show any signs of wavering. "OK," he finally said.

"OK what?"

"OK, we're good."

"Just like that?" I snapped my fingers. "You're not going to make me beg?"

"Do you want to beg?"

"Not particularly."

"Then we're good. Make sure you aren't legally married to Kevin, please."

I gave him a captain salute.

"Is there *anything* else you need to tell me?" he asked.

"No." I paused to think. "Right, no."

He bent down and pressed his lips against my cheek, brushing it lightly, sending shivers through my nerves. When he finally kissed my mouth, it was like everything had gone quiet. Like our problems had slipped away, and all that mattered was that he and I were standing there in the middle of the—

Honk!

We jumped back. Daniella sat at the helm of her car, laying on the horn.

Hoooonnnnk!

She poked her head out the window. "Find a room!"

Chase waved. "Have a good morning."

Daniella showed him her middle finger.

"Like I said, I'd be a raging alcoholic if I had your job." He gave me a peck on the cheek. "And remember, we have dinner tomorrow night with Silvia and Hampton."

Oh, hell.

CHAPTER TWENTY-ONE

Detail oriented

I went back into my apartment and found Amy and Tom on the couch with Munch, who was lying with his belly up, tongue out, and he was wiggling around to make sure he left behind as much hair as possible. Kevin was sitting at the kitchen table next to Lilly, who was dressed like the Hulk, and the two were eating sparkle toast.

"For the record," I heard Amy saying as I walked past them to the kitchen, "Chase has far better taste in rings."

Oh, geez.

"You doing all right?" I sat beside Kevin and placed my good hand over his.

"Situation sucks."

"That it does. What happens now?" I paused to sneeze. "Trevor gets everything and hires a new management company?"

"Why would he hire a new management company?"

That's right, I hadn't told him about Patrick quitting. So I did.

"Not surprised. He could never hang," he said. "If you don't get the job next door now, then you're screwed."

"What does screwed mean?" Lilly asked.

I licked my thumb and wiped jam from her face. "It means someone is in big doo-doo."

Lilly pushed my hand away. "You're in doo-doo?"

"Don't worry about Mommy. I'm good."

Lilly smiled and scooted off to say good-bye to Tom and Munch. I waved from my spot at the table, too tired to stand.

My cell rang from my purse on the counter. I contemplated letting the call go to voice mail. Surely falling from a burning building warranted a day off—or ten. I was almost out of sick days, but what was Patrick going to do? Fire me?

Well, actually, I supposed he could. He *was* still my boss, and it wasn't like he was going to walk away from Elder Property Management tomorrow. My contract stated that I had to give thirty days. Surely he'd have to give Trevor at least that long to find a new management company. Or not. Honestly, I had no idea.

Really, I should just answer the phone.

I stood at the counter and dug my cell out of my purse. Crap. It was the Dashwoods. "This is Cambria," I answered with as much cheer as I could muster.

"Cambria, Patricia Dashwood here. I don't want to beat around the bush. I've called to thank you for interviewing for the management position. Unfortunately, we cannot offer you the job."

I stared down at my phone in bewilderment. Had she really just said that I didn't get the job?

"Cambria? Are you there?"

"Yes." I came to. "I'm sorry. Can I ask why?" Not that I had to. She'd obviously heard about the girl in the barrel and the McMillses. A triple homicide and burned down mansion in Brentwood was newsworthy. I was sure there were reporters standing outside the Burbank building, harassing my residents as they came to and from their apartments, wanting their opinion on the scandal.

"Dependability is what we were looking for in our new manager."

Wait…what? "Dependability?" I repeated.

"Reliable." Kevin approached. "Trustworthy. Steadfast. Loyal."

Loyal? I was the most loyal person I knew! "What makes you think I am not dependable?"

"I still don't have your resume."

Oh, no. She was right. I was supposed to bring it with me to the interview, but the goat had eaten it. Then I was supposed to email it to her, but I was distracted by murder. "Are you sure this doesn't have to do with what happened at our Burbank property?"

"I'm not sure what you're talking about."

My stomach plunged into my gut with the realization that I'd managed to screw myself out of this job. It had nothing to do with the woman in the barrel. Crap! My plan was to secure the job and ask that Mr. Nguyen be given a position on the maintenance team. I'd let us both down. "I'm so sorry, Dr. Dashwood. Would you reconsider if I sent the resume now?"

"Thank you for interviewing with us." Her tone was polite but implacable.

"Thank you." I put the phone down and buried my head in my hands. "I didn't get the job." I kept my voice low, not wanting Lilly or Amy to hear. Not ready to tell them there would be no pay increase or vision or high-rise or wow fridges or theater room or game room or conference room or *any* room. I was about to be homeless.

Kevin poked me with the tip of his finger. "Are you going to cry?"

"No." *Well, maybe.*

Amy screamed. Both Kevin and I looked out to the living room, where she was jumping around with her phone at her ear. "Thank you. Thank you. Thank you!" she squealed. "Thank you! Thank you! Bye!" She threw her arms up in the air and continued to hop around as if she'd just been called down as a contestant on the *Price is Right.*

Lilly stared at me. "What's wrong with hers?"

No idea.

Amy scooped up Lilly and spun her around the room. "I scored an audition for the Zankla movie!"

I brought my hand to my mouth. "Are you serious?"

"Yes! Not even for the best friend, but for *Zankla.* Reena asked for me specifically."

OK, I was in serious financial doo-doo, but this had to be celebrated.

And celebrate we did.

If celebrating meant screaming. We did a lot of screaming. Screaming was about all I could afford to do. Also, ice cream. We ate ice cream.

"Cheers." Lilly lifted her non-dairy scoop of vanilla on a cone, and we all tapped our spoons together.

"Cheers," I said and looked down at the ice cream in front of me. On second thought, I was not hungry. Not at all.

Neither was Kevin.

Or Amy.

Really, Lilly was the only one celebrating with ice cream.

"I want a DNA test," Kevin said out of the blue. "I don't think Trevor and I are related."

And...we're back to that.

"Why don't you take him up on the offer to work for him?" I asked. "You might end up getting along."

Kevin stuck his finger down his throat.

Guess that's a no.

Lilly polished off her ice cream. "Can I go change?"

"Sure."

"Yay." She hopped down and ran to her room, slamming the door behind her.

I heaved a sigh and rubbed my eyes.

"Trevor is my father's brother's son from his first marriage," Kevin continued, answering a question we hadn't asked. "There's a chance my aunt had an affair, and Trevor and I share zero blood. He used to be cool. A total brown-noser, kiss up, sycophant, bootlicker twerp. But not unbearable. As soon as he took over as the trustee, he started all this foo-foo energy weirdness." He shuddered. "The thought of working with him makes me want to gag, barf, vomit, puke, and die."

"I like him."

"*Whhhyyyy*? He's so not genuine. All his energy crap is a total act."

"It is not," Amy said defensively. "How do you think I managed to land an audition for the biggest movie on the planet? I put my desire into the Universe and the Universe provided. That's how energy works."

If that's how it works then:

Dear Universe,

I want a job with higher pay, better bonuses, and vision.

Sincerely,

Cambria Clyne

"You're as crazy as he is." Kevin pushed his bowl away.

I paused to sneeze. "If you give him a chance, you two could have a wonderful relationship."

"Maybe." Kevin coughed into the crook of his elbow. "So, how do you all think my mom killed my mom?"

"The medical examiner said she'd taken a blow to the head. What I don't get is where they were when it happened."

"The attic," Amy said. "Even I know that."

"Why were they *in* the attic, though? Was Kevin's bio mom like, *'I want to see my kid'* and Mom McMills was like, *'Sure, he's in the attic, come on up,'* and then Mom McMills clocked her on the head?"

Kevin rolled his eyes. "She killed her somewhere else then dragged her up there, *obviously.*"

"Why the heck would she hide the body in the attic? More importantly, *how* the heck did she drag a dead body up into the attic?"

"That is a good question. Mom McMills has a bad knee," he said. "Always has. She must have lured her up into the attic."

True. Or, "She had help with the body."

"My dad?"

"Your dad looked genuinely surprised that Larissa was dead."

"Patrick?"

"Sure, but why would he? What's in it for him?"

"He made money from managing the properties."

This was true. "You'd think he would have removed *all* the barrels instead of hiding just one. Who else would have helped her? Who had skin in the game?"

"Me," said Kevin.

Amy gasped. "Did *you* help hide the body?"

"Nope. I had serious drug problems back then, but I'd remember moving a dead body."

Huh? "Did your parents send you here before or after they hired Patrick?"

"After."

"Before or after they decided to make Trevor the trustee?"

"After. My mother sat me down and told me that I was a disgrace to the family name, and she told me they had decided to let Trevor have everything. I could continue to live here, rent free, so long as I never contacted them."

Geez. Harsh. "Wait, they had sent you here but were still in contact?"

"At first, yes. They just wanted me out of their house because I was bringing around questionable company. Mostly drug dealers and prostitutes."

"When did she tell you about Trevor?"

"Right before Thanksgiving. No matter how badly I'd screwed up, I never thought they'd disinherit me. They'd told me the point of all the therapy and tough love was to groom me to take over one day. Liars."

"Bet that put a damper on the holidays," said Amy.

Hold on. "According to May, a former resident who liked to peek into the attic, the barrels were moved in September. The fight between Patrick and Larissa happened in September as well. Trevor said he moved the barrels after he found out he'd be taking over the trust."

"You're saying he knew in September?"

My mind spun this information around. "Or he had reason to move the barrels and lied to us."

"My, how quickly you are to change your tune," Kevin almost sang. "I thought you liked Trevor?"

I thought I did, too.

"Pretty sure hiding a dead body is a crime," said Amy.

"I *know* it's a crime." And a *serious* accusation. Would make sense as to why they handed down their fortune to Trevor. He knew too much. Otherwise, why make such a drastic decision. It wasn't like they were on their deathbeds, and Kevin was still young.

"There's only one choice." Kevin slid his chair back. "We have to confront him."

"I am not confronting anyone."

"Yes, you are."

"No, I am not."

CHAPTER TWENTY-TWO

———

Excellent judge of character

Turns out I was.

By the time we got to Trevor's office, the receptionist was gone for the day. Good. Or bad. A third witness wouldn't hurt. I could hear Trevor behind the sheer partition in the office. He was humming.

"Hello?" I said and stepped around to find him meditating.

He was on the floor with his legs crossed, hands up over his head, eyes closed, and a blunt waiting for him in an ashtray.

Kevin clapped loud enough to make me jump. "Yo, we're here!"

Trevor's eyes popped open and he smiled. "Cousin." He rose to his feet and gave Kevin a hug and kissed me on each cheek. "So happy to receive your call and to know that you've changed your mind."

"I am so excited to work with you." Kevin could not have sounded more monotone if he tried. "Thank you for meeting me at your office."

I exhaled, making an involuntary raspberry sound. "What exactly did you have in mind for Kevin?" I asked.

"Excellent question," said Trevor. "I just heard from Patrick that he is closing up shop, which leaves us in quite the predicament. This means a lot more work. What I need is someone to run errands and make sure my fridge is stocked."

My mouth dropped open. "You want Kevin to be your personal assistant?"

"I like to think of it as my personal associate."

Kevin blinked. "That. Sounds. Good. When. Do. I—oh, hell. I can't do this. Did you help Dolores stash my real mom's body in a barrel?"

I smacked my forehead. The plan was for Kevin to strike up friendly conversation with Trevor, gain his trust, get him relaxed, and then slyly ask about the timing of everything. The hope was to get him flustered in the chance he'd accidentally incriminate himself.

"I would *never* do such a thing," Trevor said. "I am insulted by the very accusation. I do not think we should work together."

"Yeah, me either." Kevin gave him a captain salute using his middle finger.

I decided to step in. "You said that you moved the barrels when you found out that you'd be the trustee over the property. I have a resident who said the barrels were moved in September. We just pulled the paperwork this morning, and it said that the trust was not formed until November."

Trevor took a drag of his blunt and blew a marijuana cloud out in my face. I coughed and covered my nose. "They told me before they did the paperwork," said Trevor.

"They hired Patrick in September," I said. "And they didn't tell him about you until November. I'm trying to figure out why they wouldn't have told him if you were doing a tour of all properties. Seemed like something they'd mention."

Trevor brushed off my concerns with a wave of his hand. "You've been through too much. The stress is getting to you, and you're looking for problems that aren't there."

"No, she is not," said Kevin. "Dolores killed my mother, and you hid the body."

Trevor stubbed his blunt and exhaled a cloud of smoke. "What's your point? It's my word against yours."

Kevin pulled out his phone. "No. It's your word against yours. I've been recording this conversation."

Trevor yanked the phone from Kevin's hand and dropped it into a cup of water.

Well, that sucks.

"Now it's my word against yours." Trevor shook his head. "I've tried *so* hard to make this right, and you have done nothing but be a royal pain in my—"

"How have you made this right?" Kevin interrupted. "That was my real mother. That was my inheritance. You think allowing me to shop for you makes this right?"

"I am at peace!" Trevor snapped.

Wow. I'd never seen him so unhinged.

He smoothed down the white smock he was wearing and rolled his shoulders. "I am at peace," he said more even toned. "I did not kill anyone. What I did was help a family member out. That is what family does."

Not necessarily. "Did you blackmail your aunt into leaving you her fortune?" I put two and two together, realizing Trevor had enough information to ruin Dolores McMills. Even if she didn't like to part with her money, she'd been willing to pay off Larissa to make that problem go away. Why wouldn't she have done the same for Trevor?

"It's not like Kevin was fit for the job," he said. "He took up so much of their time, they had to hire a management company. With me in the picture, they could relax and enjoy life."

Kevin punched Trevor in the face. Trevor stumbled back and touched his nose, marveling down at the red coating his fingers.

"I think we're done." I grabbed Kevin's arm. "We're good."

"No." Trevor pulled a small revolver from under the beanbag. "I had a feeling you two didn't want to meet up to discuss Kevin working for me. Not after everything that happened last night. It's a damn shame." He clicked his tongue. "I really liked you, Cambria. And Kevin, I was beginning to tolerate you. I'm sorry your mother chose me over you. Get over it."

Kevin and I raised our uninjured arms up in the air. "The only reason she chose you was because you blackmailed her," Kevin said.

"Tomayto, tomahto." Trevor cocked the revolver.

Yeah, OK. I'm done.

"Abort! Abort!" I screamed. "Abort!"

The door to Trevor's office kicked in, and in came Chase, Hampton, and several other of LAPD's finest with their guns drawn. "Drop your weapon!" Chase said.

Trevor's face drained of all color, and he lowered the revolver to the ground and raised his hands up. Hampton swung Trevor's hands behind his back and slapped cuffs on his wrists. "You are under arrest for being an accessory to a crime…"

Chase escorted Kevin and me to the front lobby. "Are you two all right?"

I nodded and grabbed the mic pack tucked into the back of my pants.

"I'm grateful you called me instead of confronting Trevor on your own," said Chase, taking the microphone from my shaky grasp. "You made the right decision."

"I still think I could have taken him alone," said Kevin. "She's the one who was like *'We need to get the police involved. I'm not taking any more unnecessary risks with my life…blah, blah, blah'.*"

That was more or less how the conversation went.

Hampton paraded Trevor down the hall and to the elevator. Kevin and I took the stairs. Riding in a little box suspended above the ground was beyond my current mental capacity. My nerves were shot.

Outside the building, Hampton pushed Trevor's head down and helped him into the back of a patrol car with the lights on and flashing. He slammed the door shut, tapped the roof, and the squad car was off.

I blew out a breath. It was finally over. The McMillses were dead. Trevor was on his way to jail… Wait a second. "Kevin, does this mean *you* now get everything?"

He shrugged, as if the thought had not occurred to him. "Don't you wish you would have signed the marriage certificate?"

No. Maybe. Wait, no. Definitely no.

"Guess that means I'm now your boss." Kevin swung his good arm over my shoulders. "Make me a sandwich, woman."

"Make it yourself."

Hampton sauntered up, giving his pants a hike. "You two did a good job."

"Thank you," I said.

Chase squeezed my arm. "I'm thinking since you're injured and have been through so much that it would be best if we reschedule our dinner plans."

Hallelujah! I do love this man.

Hampton gave an understanding nod of his head. "Of course. Silvia will absolutely understand. She's a very compassionate person."

Kevin coughed to cover a laugh.

"When would be a better time?" Hampton asked.

I was about to say my schedule looked good the year after next, when Chase said, "With me leaving soon, it's too hectic. Let's plan on when I get back."

FBI training was four months. Fewer than two years, but still not tomorrow, so I was happy.

"It's a plan." Hampton thanked Kevin and me again for our help, then stepped away to call Silvia and break the news.

"Can you give us a minute?" Chase asked Kevin.

Kevin rolled his eyes. "Fine. So long as you talk loud enough so I can hear from over there." He pointed to the spot near the door where he'd presumably be standing and eavesdropping.

"I'll try my hardest," Chase said.

Kevin left, and Chase moved his hands up to my face, cradling my cheeks, rubbing my skin with his thumbs. "Thank you again for calling me instead of confronting Trevor on your own."

"I promised I'd be safe."

Chase's eyes slid down to the splint on my wrist.

"That was *not* my fault. I was pushed out the window—"

Chase pressed his mouth against mine, and I forgot what I was saying. His arms wrapped themselves tightly around me, and I rose to my toes. I closed my eyes and lost myself in his touch. Everything in my body told me this was right. He tasted right. He smelled right. Even the roughness of his five o'clock shadow on my skin felt right. I wanted to bottle these feelings up and carry them around with me for the next four months.

CHAPTER TWENTY-THREE

———

Dependable

Chase left on a Tuesday. We said good-bye at the airport, and I cried the entire way home. Kevin and Amy and Lilly were waiting for me with ice cream and donuts and *Law and Order* reruns and Kleenex and hugs. Lots and lots of hugs.

Two months later, and life had returned to somewhat normal. Chase and I talked once a day, even if it was for only a few minutes. Keeping the flame alive long-distance was harder than I'd anticipated. Training was difficult, and Chase was exhausted. Our conversations had gotten shorter and shorter with each passing day. But I refused to give up on us.

Good thing I had work to keep me busy. With the McMillses no longer alive and Trevor behind bars, Kevin was set to inherit everything. At least, we thought so. He was still going through probate court, and all properties sat in limbo. Luckily, Patrick agreed to stay on until the case was settled. When asked if he'd reconsider retiring, he'd said, "You couldn't pay me enough to work for another McMills." And he meant it. Kevin had offered him almost double what he was making before, and he respectfully declined by saying, "Hell, no."

Until the McMills's assets were finalized, Patrick kept his word to stay on, and we chugged along as best we could. Which meant sticking to our monthly meetings and property tours. It was a Wednesday. Lilly was at school, and I was wiping down the coffee table in the lobby. I had no idea what exactly would happen to me once Kevin regained control of his parents' property portfolio. "Whatever management company I hire will have to keep you. It will be part of the deal," Kevin had said. A beautiful gesture, but I'd been sending out my resume anyway. All positions I'd applied for were for either less money or an assistant management position. Yes, a downgrade. But I didn't want to put all my eggs in one basket. What if probate court decided Kevin didn't inherit everything? A lower-paying job was better than no job.

At least that was what I kept telling myself.

I finished wiping down the table, fluffed the pillows, and grabbed a piece of lint off the floor. Even if Patrick was only my temporary boss, I still wanted everything to look perfect. I took pride in my work, because I was dependable like that.

P.S. Still a little bitter about that.

P.P.S. Fine, a lot bitter.

The news didn't even pick up the McMills and Larissa story. Not even a three-second blip on a local station. Absolutely nothing! News of a senator who had been caught cheating, and a production company that had been caught stealing, and a tax increase, dominated the headlines. Also, there was the big cast reveal of the Zankla movie coming out next year. Everyone was talking about the seemingly unknown actress who had been cast as the lead: Amy Montgomery.

I was so proud. She'd put her wish into the Universe, and the Universe delivered.

The Universe must not have received my wish.

I went outside to check on the landscaping and make sure there wasn't any trash on the lawn. Everything looked good, except for the goat eating the grass. "You've got to be kidding me!"

The goat looked up and screamed. I knew that scream, and I knew that goat.

"Fox!" I called out. "Fox! Where are you?" I plucked the little brown goat off the ground and shoved her under my arm. "Fox!" He'd moved out last month and taken his two goats with him. He had claimed the reason he had to leave was because of the stress living there had caused him. Which could have been true, but I'd also given him a notice to vacate. So there was that.

"There you are." Fox approached with the little white goat trotting beside him on a leash. "Cambria, what are you doing here?"

"I also manage this building."

Fox looked around. "It's nice. Do you have any one bedrooms available?"

"This is a no pet property as well."

"The no pet rule is inhumane."

I tried not to roll my eyes but was only partially successful. "What are you doing here?"

"I am going next door. I'm now a certified goat yoga instructor."

"They offer yoga classes for their residents?"

"Yes, the manager there heads it up."

The new manager's name was Karan. She'd come over to introduce herself when she started. She was about my age, had a thin face, blonde hair always smoothed into a stylish bun, and a mega-watt smile with teeth so white it almost hurt my eyes. I wanted to like her, but there was something prohibiting me. It was probably the way she kept saying, "Isn't your place *so* quaint."

Anyway.

"Karan does the classes with us," Fox said. "Said it's part of her job."

Part of her job?

Oh!

My mind flashed back to my conversations with Mrs. Dashwood. *Are you comfortable with heat, or should we do smaller sizes?* She must have been talking about yoga! It's no wonder Mr. Dashwood didn't think any manager would agree.

As far as I was concerned: bullet dodged.

OK, that wasn't true. I'd let a goat climb on my back if it meant job security and vision. I really had my heart set on vision.

I said good-bye to Fox and the goats, grabbed a discarded Coke can out of the bush, and went inside to wait for Patrick. He arrived at 1:45 p.m., exactly two hours after our scheduled meeting time. Even if he had stayed on, he'd mentally checked out.

"Front looks good." He sat on the couch and placed his briefcase on the coffee table. "Did I show you the motor home we bought?"

"Yes, a few times," I said, sliding into the seat beside him.

"Has four pop outs, and three televisions."

"So I've heard."

"And we bought a Jeep." He swiped on his phone's screen and showed me a picture of a bright red off-roading Jeep. Patrick and his wife had decided to sell their home and travel across the country. Not a bad retirement plan.

"We still have the one vacancy?" he asked, trying really hard to care.

"We're full here, and we have the one at Burbank. Fox's old apartment. I know I've brought this up before, but I really think it would benefit us greatly if we added window air conditioners to the units. With no laundry and no parking available, we need at least one extra amenity to make it worth the rent."

"Go ahead."

I wasn't sure I'd heard him right. "Go ahead and get them?"

"Might as well do it now. Better to ask forgiveness than permission."

Wow. I really liked retired Patrick.

"I've been thinking, Cambria." Patrick sat back and crossed one leg over the other. "Should Kevin inherit all this"— he made a sweeping gesture to the room—"he's going to need an excellent management company to prohibit him from going bankrupt and destroying everything his parents built. Someone he trusts. Someone he listens to. Someone who is knowledgeable and dependable."

"I absolutely agree."

"I think that someone is *you.*"

"You think I should have a management company?"

"I'll be happy to get you started. I'm not going to lie—it's a soul-sucking business, and I've hated every second. But you seem to enjoy it. Imagine all the dead bodies you'll find."

"Fox. Found. Larissa." Honestly. I was about ready to tattoo this on my forehead.

"Did they ever confirm it was Larissa?"

"Yes, they did. Chase had to tell her aunt. She took the news hard, but she was happy to have answers. She and Kevin plan to meet soon."

"Hopefully he'll get one sane relative out of this mess."

My thoughts exactly. "If you're being serious about helping me form a management company, I will absolutely take you up on the offer. But what about insurance and housing and…everything?"

"If you can secure the McMillses properties, that's enough right there to line your pockets, pay for your own house, and your own insurance."

Holy hell.

Thank you, Universe.

"I'm pretty sure Kevin would hire my management company," I said. "And Tom could help me with legal stuff."

"You're resilient, Cambria. I think you'd be great. There's just the matter of stability."

"What do you mean?"

"If you created your own company here in Los Angeles, it's not going to be easy to up and move should you need to."

Oh. That. He was talking about Chase. After he finished his training, he could be assigned *any*where. That was certainly something to think about.

…

…

…

OK.

That's enough thinking.

"I want to do it," I said. "I'm tired of living in limbo. I want to work for myself and build something worth passing down to my daughter."

"Then talk to Kevin, and I will absolutely help you."

By the time our meeting was over, I'd already created my company name: Clyne Property Management—because I'm creative like that.

I didn't want to get ahead of myself. My entire business plan revolved around Kevin inheriting his parents' property portfolio, and him agreeing to hire me.

But Clyne Property Management had a nice ring to it.

Later that night, I sat on my couch in a silent room watching the clock. Kevin should have been there any minute.

The season premiere of *If Only* was on, and we wanted to watch it live.

I'd spent hours typing up a business plan for Clyne Property Management. Then I'd sent it off to Staples to be bound and spiraled, and I had it sitting on my lap, ready to present.

There was a knock on the door, and I took a deep breath, exhaled slowly, and clutched my business proposal. *You've got this, Cambria.* I crossed the room and swung open the door.

"Tom? What are you doing here?" He had on his suit and tie, and Lilly was asleep in his arms.

"I have a client who needs me right now. Third time arrested this month."

"Here. Let me have her." I set my proposal on the TV stand and took Lilly from his arms. She transferred without waking, and I carried her to her room. She rolled into bed without so much as a word, and I tiptoed out, leaving the door opened a crack, turned off the lights, and went back to the living room.

"What is this?" Tom asked, my business proposal in hand. "Clyne Property Management?"

"Patrick said I should start my own management company."

"Do *you* think you should start your own management company?" He flipped through the pages. "When did you do all this? There's like seventy pages here."

"I wanted to be thorough. And I did it this afternoon." I'd found a business proposal outline online and followed it almost exactly. Mostly. I may have expanded a few sections because I'm an over-explainer. It's what I do.

"This is a great idea, Cambria." Tom handed me back the proposal. "I'm proud of you."

"Thank you. I'm excited."

"What does Chase think?"

"I haven't told him yet. We were supposed to talk today, but he has a big test tomorrow. I'll tell him when there's something worth telling. There are a few things that need to fall into place first. Speaking of proposals. Hold on." I hurried down the hall and grabbed Tom's ring out of my suitcase.

Note to self: Unpack already. It's been two months.

Tom was shaking his head as soon as I walked into the room. "I don't want it back."

"You could return it to the store." I held the box out.

"No. I gave it to you."

"Yes, and I told you no. A few times, actually."

"Cambria, I meant every word I said. I'm not taking that ring back."

"So I'm just supposed to keep it forever? Tom, that's ridiculous."

"You never know what the future holds."

No, I didn't. I was confident that my future didn't involve adding Dryer to my last name. I mean, I was pretty confident.

Oh, hell.

Tom was staring down at me with his hazel eyes and his flirty side-smirk, and my stomach went haywire. "Time to go." I pushed him towards the door. "Good luck with your criminal. Tell him to stop breaking the law."

"I'm going to wear you down, Cam. You know it."

"No, you're not." I thrust the little box into his hands and closed the door.

Honestly, that man was infuriating. I hated that he had that effect on me.

There was another knock on the door. I checked the peephole to make sure it wasn't Tom. Oh good, Kevin! *You are dependable, hard-working, smart, business savvy, and capable,* I chanted to myself as I opened the door.

"Hello, Kevin. Please enter." I swept my hand out like I was welcoming royalty.

Kevin hesitated. "What is wrong with you?"

"Nothing at all. I'm grand."

Kevin stepped inside and checked over his shoulder. "Why is your apartment so clean?"

"Because I'm organized and efficient."

"What happened? Wait…did you get knocked up?"

"What? No. Why would you think that?"

"I don't know. Your gut looks bigger, and you're acting strange."

I sucked in my gut and closed the door. "I am not knocked up. Thank you very much. But I do have a proposal for you."

"I already married you once. Not doing it again." He plopped down on the couch. "Where's the ice cream?"

Oh, right. I hurried to the kitchen and grabbed the pecan praline from the freezer— Kevin's favorite flavor—and scooped us each a helping. "Here you go." I handed him the bowl.

"What's that tucked under your arm?"

"Oh, this?" I held out the proposal. "I've had a crazy idea. Of course, it'll depend on what the probate court says—"

"Everything is mine." Kevin sat back with his ice cream, as if it were no big deal. "Found out this morning. There's some inheritance tax crap, trust crap, and a whole bunch of legal crap. But it's all mine. Now, sit down so we can start."

"Kevin, that's wonderful. Congratulations."

"Yeah, yeah." He grabbed the remote and turned on the television.

"Before we start, I want to talk about my management company."

"When did you start a management company?"

"I haven't yet. But I want to, and I want you to hire me. It's all in here." I held up my proposal.

Kevin snatched it from my grasp, looked at the cover, and tossed it to the other side of the couch. "You're hired. Stop talking, and let's watch."

"You don't even want to read it?"

"Nope." He shoved a spoonful of ice cream into his mouth and patted the spot next to him. "Sit, Clyne."

I lowered to the couch with my bowl of ice cream in my hands. "You sure you'll hire me?"

Kevin rolled his eyes. "I already told you yes. You're one of two people I trust in the world."

"Who is the other one?"

"Your kid. She's a straight shooter. I can appreciate that." Kevin stuck out his hand. "It's a deal, Clyne."

I slipped my hand into his and smiled. "Deal."

We shook on it then settled down to watch our favorite show. It was hard to concentrate on what was happening. My mind was too busy going over how I could make Clyne Property Management a reality. What a thrill it would be to be my own boss. What a thrill it would be to have an office and a house that didn't share walls and a 401K and employees. Instead of being a property manager, I'd have property managers working for *me*. I'd have hundreds and hundreds of residents to…deal…with…which would be a lot. But not soul-crushing.

    Right?

ABOUT THE AUTHOR

Erin Huss is a blogger and best selling author. She can change a diaper in fifteen seconds flat, is a master overanalyzer, has a gift for making any social situation awkward and yet, somehow, she still has friends. She currently resides in Southern California with her husband and five children, where she complains daily about the cost of living but will never do anything about it.

To learn more about Erin Huss, visit her online at:
https://erinhuss.com

Enjoyed this book? Check out all of the
Cambria Clyne Mysteries!

www.GemmaHallidayPublishing.com

CPSIA information can be obtained
at www.ICGtesting.com
Printed in the USA
LVHW031942171220
674449LV00006B/1294